Infection

Sean Schubert

Eloquent Books

Eloquent Books
An imprint of Strategic Book Group
P.O. Box 333
Durham CT 06422
www.StrategicBookGroup.com

ISBN: 978-1-60911-935-5

Printed in the United States of America

Book Design: Rolando F. Santos

*This book is dedicated
to my loving and supporting family —
all of you.*

I

1.

"I love coming up here. Alaska is my favorite place in the whole world." Little Martin Houser truly meant what he said when he repeated his revelation for, what seemed to be, the one-hundredth time. He loved coming to Alaska with his family. He was the only one in his class who had ever been to such a distinctly different place. At first, he didn't really know what the big deal was. It was just a place after all. The more that he heard people talk about this place, however, the more he accepted that Alaska held some kind of magic. They had come to Alaska every two or three years since he was born–meaning that he was now in Alaska for his fourth time.

They stayed in a beautiful deluxe cabin. There were three bedrooms, a large great room with an enormous stone-faced fireplace, a beautiful solarium off the main room, and indoor flushing toilet. This was an amenity that his mother had always remarked as the most important feature of the cabin. Personally, Martin didn't see the big deal. He was able to do all that he needed outside in the woods, and usually did. It had just become a part of the grand experience for him. There was a loft area above the bedrooms, electricity from a very large diesel powered generator housed in a small shack outside, and even a satellite dish for television. It was better than their house.

This was an especially good year for Martin because he had been allowed to invite a friend. The decision was, not surprisingly, made the moment the opportunity was presented to Martin. He knew exactly whom he would like to bring: Danny Mahoney.

3

It was Danny Mahoney's first trip to Alaska, but given that he was only ten years old he was years ahead of most visitors to the state, who often didn't find time in their lives to visit the state until after retirement. He and Martin were best friends from playing on the same soccer team for the past two years. Martin's family, all five of them including Martin, were nice and generous and had readily welcomed Danny to travel with them, all except Alec, Martin's older brother that is. Martin's dad, Mr. Houser, was an ordinary man of ordinary height, ordinary weight, wore ordinary clothes, had an ordinary job, and led an ordinary life. Most people would consider him average, if not a little less than average, in all things in life. He was, however, pleasant and willing to spend time with Martin and Danny and any other kids that might be around; something many adults weren't willing to do themselves. Danny liked Mr. Houser and trusted him.

Mrs. Houser, Ginny, was anything but ordinary. She was about as tall as her husband but about twice his size. She was loud and easily excited and always laughing with loud, contagious, storm bursts of laughter. She was full of life and enthusiasm. She always smelled sweet and inviting; a combination of her ample perfume and the treats that were always in her pockets, purse, hands, or mouth. At soccer games, she always brought the best after game snacks and was known for that by all the other kids on the team.

Martin's brother, Alec, was older by five years, tall, thin, and athletic. He played basketball all the time and teased Martin and Danny for being too short to play basketball and had to settle with playing soccer of all things. In public, Martin and Danny both chafed at the insults and resented Alec, but in private they both secretly admired him and looked up to him. That admiration made it that much harder to accept Alec's barbed comments. Alec didn't wear really baggy clothes like a lot of his friends wore, or, more to the point; his parents wouldn't let him wear clothes like that. He compromised though by wearing a series of loose fitting licensed replica basketball jerseys and buying his jeans a size too big. That was as baggy as it got with him, which was just fine as far as he was concerned. It was harder to play a sudden impromptu game if he was wearing baggy jeans.

Martin's sister, Julie, or Jules as everyone called her, was two years younger than him. Alec had heard a conversation once between his parents and some family friends in which Jules was referred to as a mistake. Jules was small and pretty with longish dark hair and blue eyes that usually precipitated second and sometimes a third look from people. Her eyes were absolutely electric with life. Jules usually tagged along with Martin and Danny, which was just fine with them. She made the two of them three.

The three of them were running a roughly cut path through small trees and thick brush. Below them and to their right was a gray and gravelly creek bed through which coursed an equally gray and gravelly near frigid stream of melting glacial water.

To Martin, the only one of the three of them who could credibly claim to remember, it seemed that they should have already found the glacier. Had it melted? Was it all gone? He bragged about his experiences on and around this small arm of the Crenshaw Glacier. Now, with the glacier gone, would it appear that he had been only telling stories? Lies? Nervously, he started chewing on his lower lip as he ran. Where was it?

And then, there it was; part of it anyway. He could see a narrow spit of ice that thrust itself into the flowing water, as if it were the glacier's tongue lapping at the currents. Around a bend in front of them, he could finally see a substantial sea of dirty frosty white against a backdrop of green and brown. When they got closer, they could see the deep blue hue of the dense ice as it refracted the sun's light.

"What's that smell?" crowed Jules through her sudden grimace.

It was an awful odor, worse than manure smell from back home in Minnesota and worse than that rotten fish smell at the piers down in Seward. A faint breeze helped to thin it enough to continue.

Danny suggested, "Smells like somethin' died. We probably oughta watch out for bears."

Almost on cue, both Martin and Danny took their small pocketknives from their front pockets and bared their shiny blades. Jules picked up a stick and carried that at the ready.

"What's that?" asked Jules, pointing at a black mass partially encased in the receding ice.

5

"Probably where that smell is comin' from," Martin thought out loud.

And then they did what kids do. They went down to the dark mass and closer to the odor to investigate and possibly poke it with Jules' stick. Down near the creek bed and without the benefit of the breeze, the odor was all but unbearable.

Jules, through her hand cupped over her nose and mouth, said, "It looks like a person."

Danny continued her thought for her, "It does kind of look like a person. But how could a person be in the middle of this big hunk of ice?"

Martin suddenly lit up with delight. "Maybe it's a caveman or something. Maybe we're gonna be famous. Jules, you got your camera with you?"

Proud of herself for being prepared to contribute to their fame, she beamed, "Sure do," and produced the silver digital camera from her backpack.

Danny asked, "How long d'ya think it's been in there?"

Trying to sound authoritative and intelligent, Martin posited, "He's probably been in there since the last ice age. Probably thousands of years."

Jules echoed, "'Thousands of years.'"

Danny walked up and looked a little closer at the exposed upper torso, upper arms from the shoulders down to just above the elbows, and head. He had no hair and didn't appear to have any clothes. His skin was as grey as a stormy sky, with blue veins that crackled across his arms like lightning. On the left side of his neck was a terrible tear in the grey flesh that exposed the black tissue underneath. "Looks like he's really starting to rot. Maybe something took a bite outta him too."

By this time, Jules had started taking pictures. Danny, getting his nerve up a little, stood right next to the find and smiled for a snap. With the blue-white flash of the camera still spreading itself out over and around the glacier like an echo, Danny was forced to duck out of harm's way as Martin swung Jules' stick at him. The blow went wide and landed on the ice just to the left of their caveman.

Jules' begged, "Careful Marty, you might hurt him or something. Maybe we should go get mom and dad."

"Okay, but if Alec is there we don't tell him. Deal?"

The other two agreed enthusiastically.

Martin, as a last measure of his feat, decided that he too should be photographed next to their find, if only for posterity's sake. He walked over and stood right next to the frozen figure and smiled. It was a big cheesy smile that stretched all the way from their home in the Midwest to there in Alaska.

Jules held the camera up and thought she saw something that was just out of the digital frame. She lowered the camera and looked more closely. Nothing. Lifting the camera back up, she snapped another picture. But this time, as the flash momentarily partially blinded everyone, something did move. At first, Martin thought that it was just Danny swinging the same stick at him, but when the teeth came down on his shoulder he knew better.

The bite didn't break through his two shirts, but when Martin recoiled and raised his hand to fend off the attack he squealed out in pain. The frozen man was lunging desperately, hungrily at Martin. And when he got hold of Martin's hand, he bit down hard, driving one of his few jagged, brown teeth into Martin's soft, white skin.

His movements became more frantic, as he obviously tried to free himself and keep a tight hold of Martin's hand. Danny came to the rescue, striking at the man's head until he forced it to loosen its grip. Seemingly enraged, Martin's attacker started to literally quake in the icy grip that still held it firmly, if temporarily, in place.

Martin fell onto his back on the grey, silty beach. He was clutching at his hand and crying pitifully, with blood spilling onto his other hand and down his front, individual spots of crimson gradually forming into a single dark patch that covered his grey Alaska t-shirt. Danny, still holding the stick at the ready, said over his shoulder, "Jules, get him to his feet and let's get going. Jules, now."

Shaken from her stupor, Jules gathered Martin up to his feet and helped him up onto the ledge overlooking the creek. Danny was quickly on their heels, with stick still in hand.

Martin trailed blood and tears all the way back to the cabin. Even before they had gotten there, Danny started yelling at the top of his voice. He shouted for help, any help that he could get for his friend who was starting to stagger slightly.

Mr. Houser was the first to get to them, running to meet their voices just outside the clearing where the cabin sat. Ginny, Martin's mother, was standing in the doorway, looking out with concern. In her hand, she still held the knife with which she was cutting the watermelon she was preparing for a snack.

She yelled from the door, "What happened Marty?"

He stuttered, "...bit me. He bit me. I can't believe it. He bit me."

Mr. Houser looked to Danny for clarification, "What's he talking about?"

He didn't realize how ridiculous it sounded until after he had said it, but Mr. Houser's reaction to the story was enough for him to make that realization.

"Who bit Marty?"

Jules chimed in, "It's true. There was a man...a caveman frozen in the ice. And he bit Marty's hand. He must have only been sleeping when he got frozen and woke up kind of hungry. He bit Marty awfully hard."

Ginny, still in the doorway, shouted, "What happened dear?"

Mr. Houser answered flatly, "Something bit Marty."

Jules offered her correction, "A man...a caveman bit Marty." And running across the clearing toward her mother she continued, "He smelled really bad mommy. And was yucky all over." She started to cry, "And when he bit Marty, he scared me."

"Oohhhhh honey. It'll be okay. Whatever it was, is probably long gone by now. You're okay and we'll make sure Marty is okay too." Jules all but disappeared in the warm, sweet embrace of her mother, but the security therein did not stop the tears.

By then, Mr. Houser and Danny had helped Martin to the cabin. The puncture wound was a small hole in the soft tissue between Martin's thumb and index finger. To Mr. Houser, it really didn't appear to be much of an injury, but try as he might to apply pressure he couldn't stop the bleeding. He wiped the gash repeatedly but as quickly as he did, like oil seeping up through sand, the blood returned. He'd soiled a handful of towels before deciding that something else needed to be done.

Mr. Houser suggested, "I think he's bleeding pretty bad here. I think we oughta get him back to a hospital. He might need a rabies shot or something. Where's Alec?"

"He's around the other side shooting baskets."

"No, I'm not. I'm right here. Heard him crying all the way up," interrupted Alec. He looked at Marty at first with annoyance and then with genuine concern once he saw the amount and deep red of the blood that was all over his brother's shirt, pants, and arms.

"What happened to you?"

Danny told Alec all of what happened, fully expecting some snide comment that would undoubtedly be tied to their age and the fact that they played soccer and were too short to play basketball. He didn't get any of that though. In fact, Alec merely nodded his head and started to think about what could be done. He remembered the Remington .410 shotgun that was inside on top of the tall bookshelf. Maybe while everyone else was taking Marty to the hospital, he could go out toward the glacier and maybe get a little revenge. Yeah, that's what he'd do. He'd go out there and take care of...whatever was out there. How hard could it be?

2.

The trip down to the cabin had taken between three and three and half hours. They had driven at a reasonable pace; pointing out wildlife, mountains, and anything else that caught their eyes. Danny had been excited by everything. The water to his right, the Cook Inlet was what he had heard it called, was so dark and cold and calm. It wasn't anything like any of the lakes or ponds back in Minnesota. They saw white goats on the tops of the steep cliffs that bordered the twisting Seward Highway. Danny couldn't imagine how they had gotten up there in the first place. A little further down, an eternity's worth of melting running water had cut a small grotto into the rocks at the road level. In this depression was a family of three goats. The mother and two babies were only a few feet from the lanes of the highway and its rushing cars. Of course, the Housers and Danny had stopped and taken innumerable pictures. The goats didn't seem to mind really. They just went about eating the green vegetation that was growing on and amidst the rocks. That had all taken place during the early morning hours of the day, when Alaska and its majesty was just emerging and finally wiping the last of the sleep from its eyes.

It is truly amazing the differences between the sun rising and the sun falling. What Danny was coming to realize was that sunset in Alaska was very different than anything he had ever encountered. The sun was as reluctant to go to bed as his kid sister back in Minnesota, who lingered and stalled all through the house despite being told that it was time. When the sun did finally find its resting place behind the mountains to his left, there was a loitering purple hue that teased the eyes with hints of darkness without actually embracing shadows in earnest. It was dark without any real commitment.

The radio was playing some forgotten song from some guy whose name, something Diamond as he recalled, was lost on him. On the way to the cabin earlier in the day, Mr. Houser would, on occasion for specific songs, turn up the volume until Ginny would look over at him and then the volume would come back down. Now, the music was barely audible and all but ignored by everyone in the van...like a lost memory that no one missed enough to actually remember.

Like the sun, it seemed that all the animals they had seen on the trip down had found their beds for the night. There were a few birds circling and fluttering over the inlet to his left, but even they seemed to be heading for their roosts, having punched out from working an avian third shift.

He watched the last bird, a white and grey gull, circle and spin out of sight. It was then that he noticed that the inlet, earlier in the day surging and filled with white-capped dark water, was now an expanse of black sand or possibly mud. He wasn't sure of its consistency but he was certain that it looked cold and forbidding, with tiny desperate rivulets cut into its surface by separated pools of water seeking company.

Danny sat back in his seat and closed his eyes. It had been a long, tiring day. As the first gentle caress of sleep greeted him, the image of the "caveman", with his straggly long hair and bone thin grey body, splashed itself violently into the calm pool of his mind. He jolted himself forward and threw open his eyes, half fearing what he'd see. Coming in quick, shallow gasps, his breathing surprised even him. He looked around and nothing had changed except Jules. She was staring at him as if she had expected his abrupt waking.

"You saw him didn't you?"

His brow wrinkled and he searched for a response, but his tongue was too dry to form speech. For lack of words and through his still sharp breathing, Danny only nodded. He looked around for a distraction...anything. There was nothing. There was only Martin's delirium and drifts between stupor and semiconsciousness. His face was rapidly fading of any color, leaving a translucent layer of skin that didn't quite hide the pulsing blue veins just below the surface. The only color remaining in his face were two dark grey crescents forming under his swollen eyes. His pallid face glistened with sweat, though his temperature never rose above normal.

Ginny, sitting in the front seat of the rented Chevy Venture minivan, kept leaning back to the first bench seat where Martin was languishing. She was crying and quite obviously terrified. It was killing her to see her little boy suffering so much and to not be able to do anything to alleviate the pain or make him better. She wrung her hands incessantly, not knowing for sure what to do or even what she could do.

Mr. Houser didn't speak much and chose instead to focus on the road in front of him. He darted in and out of cars, sometimes skirting the right hand shoulder to get around the lumbering motor homes that dominated and were usually the cause of the long rows of traffic that choked the winding Seward Highway. Despite the traffic and the dark, Mr. Houser was doing his best to cut the drive time in any way he was able. He was desperate, as much for Ginny as for little Martin, to get his son to the hospital in Anchorage.

Jules and Danny were sitting in the bench seat furthest back in the van. Jules was crying quietly as she watched first her stricken brother, then her weeping mother, and then her intensely concentrating father. No one in their family had ever been this sick before and it scared her terribly. She leaned into Danny on more than one occasion for some comfort. She had always liked Danny, especially since he readily agreed to let her come along with Marty and him. In fact, she was pretty sure that it was Danny who convinced her brother to let her come along at all. She didn't know that for sure, but she did know that before Danny came along she had always been too young to play with Marty or tag along on any of his adventures with his other friends. Danny accepted her along and, as a result, so had Marty.

Now though, she wondered if it wouldn't just have been better had she not been along in the first place. If she weren't there with her camera, then maybe Marty wouldn't have gotten so close to the caveman and wouldn't have been bitten in the first place.

Maybe it was all her fault that this was happening.

She started to cry more loudly and said, "Momma, I'm sorry. It's all my fault that Marty is sick. It's all my fault..." Her tears and sobbing mixed with her words in a confusing mess that was all but unintelligible. Getting a concerned look from Ginny, Danny wrapped his arm around Jules and hugged her to him tightly. She kept crying into his shoulder and all that Danny could understand was the word, "camera."

3.

They got to the hospital, Providence Medical Center, and Mr. Houser scooped Martin from the back seat and carried him directly into the Emergency Room. It was busy but not overwhelmingly so. It was Sunday very late by the time they arrived and apparently injuries and sicknesses for everyone else in Anchorage had gone to bed early that night.

There was a couple with an obviously sick infant. The mother was rocking slowly back and forth, humming a tune that Danny recognized but couldn't identify. There was another woman there with her son who had a fishhook stuck all the way through his thumb. The boy was crying but it appeared that his pain was slowly losing ground to his fatigue as his eyes opened more slowly with each blink. There was a man with his foot propped up on a pile of towels stacked atop the back of one of the black synthetic leather chairs. He was reading a magazine and didn't seem to be in any undue distress. There were nurses wearing scrubs and doctors and lab technicians with all-too-familiar white lab coats walking here and there. There was activity, but nowhere near the level that Danny had associated with a typical Emergency Room. His one trip to the hospital back home was over a very busy Fourth of July weekend last summer. That was utter chaos, but nothing like the Providence Emergency Room.

Danny and Jules sat in the chairs while Ginny and Mr. Houser stood at the Nurse's Station explaining that Martin had been bitten by some wild animal and needed to be seen immediately. Seeing the wad of blood soaked towels and rags wrapped around the youngster's hand, the nurse behind the counter scribbled notes down on a piece of paper and hurried them through a pair of doors, behind which they disappeared for several minutes before Ginny reappeared to beckon Danny to bring Jules and follow her.

Most children do not feel comfortable in hospitals and Danny was no exception. The antiseptic smells, the oppressive white on the walls, beds, clothes, and even floor, and the presence of sickness all mixed to make a hospital as inhospitable a place as Danny could imagine. The three of them boarded an elevator that boasted a large letter E next to it and took it to another floor and then made their way through a series of hallways until they came to another nurse's station. They were in the Intensive Care Unit where Martin was receiving emergency and very aggressive treatment by specialists who couldn't even determine what was afflicting him.

Danny heard a couple of nurses talking to one another about Martin. They couldn't seem to figure out why he was so sick from such a small bite. At least that was what Danny understood them to be saying. He wasn't able to follow all of their words but he could certainly read their demeanor. Standing there more or less next to and sometimes in the Nurses' Station, he was starting to feel very uncomfortable.

Danny and Jules were shown to another set of black chairs and told to wait, and then Ginny scurried off down the hall and disappeared again. By that time, even the legendary midnight sun of Alaska had waned and night was fast upon the city. Jules was very quickly asleep, snoring small kazoo-like sounds from her nose. Danny stood up and stretched and realized that he was about as alone as he could get. His only company was a sleeping eight-year-old girl and his thoughts. He too was exhausted but was afraid to sleep. It was just something about hospitals.

4.

Own the hall and in one of the many rooms set aside for those patients requiring special care and attention, Ginny and Mr. Houser were talking to a doctor.

"What kind of an animal was it?"

Mr. Houser, starting to get frustrated with answering the same question over and over again, said through an aggravated sigh, "I don't know. For the thousandth time, I don't know. Marty, his sister, and his friend all wandered down to the glacier while we got ourselves situated in the cabin. While they were there, something attacked my son."

"Okay, are the other two children here in the hospital? Maybe I could get an idea of any potential toxicity from them."

"Yeah, they're down the hall. Ginny, you stay here while I take the Doc to talk to Danny and Jules."

Mr. Houser, as small as he may have been compared to his wife, wrapped her tightly in his arms and kissed her gently on the forehead. He held her against him for a time without saying a word. Then he said, "You take care of our boy and I'll be right back. Everything's gonna be fine. Okay?"

Ginny nodded through her tears and sat back down in the chair next to the bed. Martin was breathing in quick, shallow breaths. He hadn't opened his eyes in quite some time and hadn't said a word in an even longer time. The top of the sheet nearest to his face and neck was damp with sweat, as was his hair. The half-moons under his eyes had grown darker, giving the impression that his eyes were sinking deeper into their sockets.

And then Martin Houser was struggling to take in a breath. He started to shake horribly. Ginny grabbed his hand and started pleading, "Breathe Marty. Breathe. Listen to your momma. Breathe honey, please."

Unable to take her eyes away from the single bar of light that crawled across the life monitoring machinery, she shouted to the closed door, "Oh God, somebody come help me! Help my boy! Please God no! Somebody help me!" She held her son's limp hand and refused to let it go.

A nurse ran into the room and immediately checked Martin, then checked the machines to which he was attached, and then checked Martin again. "Mrs. Houser, I'm going to need you to step outside for a moment, please."

Sounding almost sick, Ginny countered, "I'm staying with my boy. He needs me. My boy needs his momma. Marty, momma's here honey. Please wake up honey. Please! Oh God, please!"

Another person and then another came in, but Ginny didn't even really notice anymore. They tried everything they could to revive little Martin. But try as they might, nothing they did seemed to work. He was absolutely unresponsive to any and all life saving procedures they attempted. His little body was just too ravaged by whatever it was that was attacking it. Luckily, it wasn't a long battle. His body merely quit and nothing seemed to matter.

Ginny, still holding Martin's rapidly cooling hand, fell onto the floor and sat there weeping. The terrible, dull, cold pain that filled her chest and fouled her stomach was like nothing she had ever known and something that she could have gone her entire life without knowing. The day and all that had happened seemed but a blur of images and then only agony. Had it only been one day? She wasn't remotely certain anymore. The one thing that she was sure of though was that her little boy was gone...forever.

One of the nurses, the first to have arrived in the room, leaned closer to Ginny and whispered, "I'm very sorry Mrs. Houser." It was then that the grief finally grabbed hold of her. Her weeping became loud sobbing. Attempts to lift her from the floor were swiped away with her moist, meaty hands. "Just leave me alone. Leave me be. Let me have a few minutes with my little boy. I only want a few more minutes with my boy."

Realizing that it would be just as well to let her calm down in the room rather than out in the hallway and risk disturbing other patients, the collection of white and blue clad medical staff all decided to leave her where she sat. Once alone, Ginny hoisted herself up and into one of the chairs in the room. She sat there quietly for several minutes while she tried to digest what had just happened. Could her little Martin be gone? Her face was hot with sorrow and tears and her head pounded painfully.

She sat there, staring blankly at the wall. When the sheet covering her now motionless Martin moved, she was startled and a little excited. Had they made a mistake? She stood up and got closer to the bed just as he sat up.

"Marty? Are you okay honey?" Standing next to his bed, Ginny leaned in and took the child in her arms. She held him tight against her, resting his head on her shoulder. She couldn't have been happier. Her boy was all right.

She didn't see him open his eyes and see the burning hunger that colored his blackened irises. She felt him move but didn't see his mouth open wide just before he dug his teeth into her throat. In terror, she tried to scream but was unable to as his jaw crushed her windpipe while he ripped huge chunks of soft white tissue from her neck. She fell backward with a look of profound astonishment across her face. Marty leapt from the bed and followed her down to the floor.

5.

Mr. Houser and Doctor Caldwell had, meanwhile, been talking to Danny about the attack and the animal that bit young Martin. Neither of the men accepted that it was a caveman of sorts that had been responsible. They asked Danny again and again in every way they could imagine to describe to them what had happened and what had done it. Nearly to tears, Danny couldn't seem to impress upon them how serious he was nor how sure he was of whom or what had bitten poor Martin.

It was Jules who came to the rescue with, "Danny's right. He's telling the truth. He's on my camera."

Mr. Houser asked, "What?"

"Go ahead. Look."

"What's on there honey?"

"He is, I think. He was too scary to look at so I just turned my camera off. But he's still on there. Go ahead, look."

Mr. Houser grabbed the camera abruptly from his daughter. He pressed the power button and the idling camera turned off and beeped: dead battery.

"Jules honey, did you actually turn the camera off?"

"Uhhhhhh. I thought I did."

"Goddamnit! D'you have the power cord?"

"Uh-huh," she said and produced the black cord from her bag.

The doctor grabbed the first hospital staffer he saw, a young Certified Nursing Assistant named Jerry. He didn't know Jerry that well, but he did know that Jerry was young and could more than likely make this camera work again.

"Take this camera and the three of them to the nearest outlet and make this thing work. As soon as you get it going, come find me. Drop everything else that you're doing and get this done now. Got it?"

The doctor didn't bother to wait for a response. He turned and was about to speak with Mr. Houser again when a nurse's scream from down the hall drew both of their attentions. It was coming from the direction of Martin's room. The two of them ran down the hall, Mr. Houser shouting to Danny, "Take care of her."

Danny nodded, though Mr. Houser was no longer facing him, and followed the new guy that was taking them to an office only two doors from where they were. Jerry fumbled with a key chain that, in Danny's estimation, probably held keys for every door in the hospital as well as Jerry's house, his car, and the doors of all of his neighbors. They rattled and jingled a song while he sought the proper key. On the other side of the door was a small office cluttered with file boxes in one corner, a computer monitor and CPU on and under the corner of a desk of sorts, and a pair of chairs that just barely fit into the small space. Jerry moved a picture frame of several someones, none of which were Jerry, and exposed a black power outlet that amazingly wasn't being used.

They all sat down, Jerry in the bigger, more plush office chair, and Danny and Jules sharing the other chair. They watched the little light on the side of the camera go from red to green in a matter of seconds. Jerry, a nineteen year old who had just earned his GED and Nursing Assistant certification a few months ago, had been working for Providence Health Systems for about six months but had just moved to the hospital from one of its long term care annexes from around the city. He was glad to have made the change. He liked what he did, even the nitty gritty of helping elderly folks dress, bathe, and care for themselves. He however found it difficult to work in a setting in which he constantly saw those for whom he had cared and grown accustomed to seeing die. He realized that was in the nature of such a facility, but it was still hard for him to get close with some of these folks only to arrive some mornings to find that Mrs. Gillum died last night or that Mr. Fredericson has elected to go home to spend his last hours with family. He wasn't prepared to be reminded of his mortality in such aggressive ways so early on in his medical career. He wanted to work somewhere that he might be able to save lives and not just to...well, not just to watch people die. It had become very depressing and he was all set to go back to work for Fred Meyer as a cashier when he was presented with the opportunity to move over to the hospital and work as a Floater, moving between departments.

He knew that helping doctors directly and getting them to know your name was one way that he might meet the right person who could help steer him toward the best opportunity to advance his career. He wanted to get a degree in the health industry, but was unsure of whether he wanted to complete a degree in Nursing or to get a series of certifications that would allow him to really diversify his worth to any hospital or medical group. He knew that he wanted to be in the medical field, he just wasn't sure in what capacity that might be. Before he started his vocational training classes, he never would have thought it possible that he would be thinking in such long term possibilities and now that was all that he could do. He finally could feel his future opening up to him and for once he was excited about something beyond next weekend.

Jerry lifted the camera, saying, "Do you mind if I have a look?"

Jules, partly surprised to have an adult ask her permission to do anything, nodded. "Go ahead."

"Okay, how do you...oh, never mind, got it," Jerry pressed two buttons and was then advancing rapidly through a day's worth of tourist photos. Barely pausing to even see the pictures as they passed, he asked, "What are we supposed to be looking for? What did the Doc want us to find?"

The next image was his answer. What he saw in that picture was frightening. "Is this real?"

Both kids nodded to him.

"Where was this?"

Jules, lifting her shoulders, said innocently, "Far away...in Alaska."

Danny added, "I think I heard something about a place called Seward somewhere close by, but I don't know for sure. This is my first time up here."

Almost as an afterthought, Jerry said absently, "Welcome to Alaska. First time, huh?

"Yeah."

Jerry couldn't change the camera's digital facade. The face contained therein was horrifying and a little familiar. He had seen faces like this one before but never in his wildest dreams did he think he would see them thus.

The face was hideously disfigured and grey, with skin stretched tightly across his cheekbones and jaw. In some places, those same bones were emerging from breaks and tears in the upper layer of tissue. There were no eyes in the empty and blackened sockets, but the face did seem to be looking, searching. His gums were the same color and seeming consistency as tar and were spread out over his few brown jagged teeth.

This wasn't a caveman as the kids had suggested, but he couldn't get his mind around what it appeared to be. Things like this existed only in horror movies or video games. He knew that for him to tell someone, anyone about his suspicions, he would first be laughed at and then sent to the lab to have a urinalysis drug screen performed. How could he possibly approach someone, especially someone of authority, and tell him that he thinks they have a zombie problem?

The screaming down the hall had intensified to an almost feverish pitch. Jerry could tell that the level of activity and, in all probability, chaos had also increased. There had been several calls for security personnel over the public address system. To the chorus of screaming had been added an accompanying rhythm of smashing furniture and a melody of shattering glass.

Instinctively, Jerry knew that he needed to get out of there. He looked at the two kids in his charge and paused. What was he to do with them? He could just say that he had to get out of there and leave them to their own luck. He could venture down that hallway and try and find their dad or at least the doctor with whom the dad seemed to be working. Or...

He looked at the little boy. "What's your name?"

"Danny."

"Where're you from Danny?"

"Minnesota."

"And how about you?" he asked looking at the cute little girl.

"I'm Julie...Jules and I'm from Minnesota too."

"You guys brother and sister?"

Danny answered, "No, I'm up here with her family on vacation before the school year starts. It was her brother who got bit and got sick."

"If it's okay with you two, we're gonna go find some place safe to wait until all the shouting has stopped. Okay?"

The shouting and screaming was moving closer down the hall. Then they heard what could only be described as a gunshot that reverberated down toward them. For a second or two, the loud resonance banging around inside their heads was all that any of them could hear.

Jerry looked one more time down the hall to try and discern if either the doctor or the dad was coming back. Scared faces hurried from the hallway, some pushing people in wheelchairs and some pushing beds and gurneys with sheet draped patients still on them. He said to the kids and to himself, "This is going to get really bad really quick. I think we better get out of here. I promise I won't let anything happen to either of you and as soon as they get all of this sorted out, we'll come back here and find your mom and dad and brother. How does that sound?"

Jules was hesitant at first until another gunshot got her back to her feet. She was ready and with that so was Danny.

6.

While Jerry, Danny, and Jules were getting the camera to work and Jerry was coming to the realization of what was happening, something very different was occurring down in Martin's room.

The initial scream that had spurred the doctor and Mr. Houser down the hall came from a nurse who had gone back into Martin's room to check on the grieving Ginny. She was not at all prepared for what she saw. Ginny was lying on her back motionless. Around her head was a pool of thick, sticky, and steadily spreading very red blood. Hunched over her was the boy that only minutes before had been declared dead. The nurse heard a horrible wet tearing sound followed by unmistakable chewing. When the little boy finally sensed the nurse's presence, he turned quickly; his face covered in the mortal soft remains of his own mother, and lunged at her.

She pushed him away desperately, screaming for help all the while. He bit her on the wrist and with surprising ease opened her radial artery and vein. The pain immediately helped her get her wits about her. She positioned her legs as she had been instructed in self-defense class, one behind the other. Then she struck her attacker with the palm of her hand, hitting him on the chest in a very powerful downward thrust. He was pushed backward and tumbled awkwardly head over heel for a moment. That was enough for her to get out and shut the door behind her.

Still leaning against the door, being nudged again and again from the other side, she applied all the pressure she could to her wrist. She slowed the bleeding somewhat, but the loss of blood was starting to make her feel weak. She was only partially coherent when all the others arrived...the doctors, the environmental techs, the other nurses...so many faces. Her consciousness was all but faded when Doctor Kozlov opened the door and released that maniacal child into the hallway. The battle. The pushing. The biting. The hitting. The beating. Less than a blur really. Cold. There was only cold now.

"Jesus Christ! What the hell was wrong with that kid?" demanded Jackson Lynus. "Man, I didn't know being a fucking security guard at the hospital meant that I was gonna be gettin' bit.

"What was wrong with that kid?"

Doctor Millenus shook his head and answered honestly, "I don't know. We pronounced him dead. He was dead. We tried to resuscitate but got nothing. It was like his body just wanted to be dead."

Lynus tucked his chin closer to his head, wrinkled his brow incredulously, and said, "You what? You mean he was...? But he was up and.... What are you trying to say? Could you've made a mistake somehow? Maybe he wasn't dead and just woke up real pissed off that you wrote him off so easy."

"No. He was dead."

"Then how the f...how do you explain this?" asked Lynus, showing the doctor his wound. "He sure bites awfully hard for a dead kid."

The sight of the security guard's wound was enough to bring the doctor back. He tried to bring order to the hallway. He needed to know whom all was hurt and then start to prioritize based upon severity of injury. He was reminded of his days as a field surgeon with the Army in Kuwait. There he had to triage dozens of men with horrible shrapnel and bullet wounds and had to do it sometimes with the sound of artillery resounding overhead.

Mr. Houser and Doctor Caldwell returned somewhere in the midst of the chaotic aftermath. When Doctor Millenus saw Mr. Houser, he realized the poor father hadn't even heard that his son had died the first time yet. The doctor was all set to deliver the terrible news and then the bizarre events following the boy's death, when Mr. Houser recognized the dead child on the floor in the middle of the hallway.

His face, chest, and legs filled with bewildering shock. He was utterly speechless, his eyes speaking volumes, asking questions, pleading for understanding. There were at least three white clad hospital employees on the floor holding white gauze to wounds on their legs, arms, and one's face. Then there was the large black security guard standing with Doctor Millenus; his hand was bleeding, but in the other he was holding a large, heavy black flashlight that was quite obviously shimmering with wetness. Mr. Houser quickly surmised that it was this man who had beaten his child to death.

He fell to his knees at his child's side, scooped the boy up in his arms, and then rolled him over onto his back. Mr. Houser recoiled in terror at the sight of his boy. The grey under his eyes had spread to most of his face while all of his veins, blue with oxygen-depleted blood, stood out like blue webbing just beneath his skin. The most startling thing though was the blood and other matter that was spread across his face, especially his mouth. He was an utter mess and barely resembled the boy who had been so excited to be in Alaska just a handful of hours ago.

Mr. Houser's weeping slackened just slightly and became concern when he realized that he didn't see his wife anywhere amongst the faces standing around him. He looked at Doctor Millenus and asked, "Where's Ginny? Where's my wife? What have you done with her?" And he shot a demanding angry look first at Doctor Millenus and then at the security guard who was even then hiding the flashlight-turned-weapon behind his leg.

Doctor Millenus had all but forgotten about the grieving mother who, to his mind, was probably still behind the closed door of the boy's former room. He looked at the door and paused. There was a smear of red, more than likely from the nurse who had first been attacked and then held the door closed until Doctor Kozlov opened it. Mr. Houser was able to surmise the doctor's thoughts and went to the door. He looked back at his dead son still lying alone in the middle of the floor and tried to figure out a way to help his wife understand what had happened.

He opened the door and saw a pool of blood on the floor and footsteps leading away from it toward the door. They were smaller footsteps, so Mr. Houser just figured those must be from

Martin. At first, he didn't see Ginny. It appeared that she had already fled the room. Maybe she was down the hall being treated herself. Who's blood was that on the floor?

Something, a kind of wet, tearing sound, drew his attention over toward the bathroom door in the corner. The door was propped open slightly and there on the floor on her knees partially in and partially out of the doorway was Ginny. It was then that he saw there was someone else there on the floor with her...under her. She was straddling a pair of legs wearing white slacks and white shoes. Ginny was grunting and breathing very deeply.

"Ginny honey, is everything okay?"

He didn't even have time to register surprise before she was upon him. They crashed against the wall with a thud that shook everyone still in the hallway outside. Doctors Millenus and Caldwell realized something was very wrong but it was too late. The first nurse that Martin had attacked and bitten on the hand shot up from the gurney on which she was laying and took hold of the orderly standing near her. Doctor Kozlov, who had been suffering horribly from the bite wound to his face, lost his balance at the same time and collapsed on the floor, convulsing as he lay dying.

He was up again before anyone was able to pry loose the orderly from the nurse's gnashing teeth. He leapt at Doctor Millenus, biting the back of the physician's neck right at the base of his skull. The doctor tried to fend off his attacker, but the teeth were driven too deeply and his arms were holding too tightly. He spun around like a bronco trying to buck its rider but the teeth dug deeper.

There was no one who could help him, as everyone around him was fighting his or her own separate battles. Orderlies and security guards were attempting to hold at bay the multiplying assailants while, at the same time, ferrying away victims suffering from multiple wounds. Several of the guards themselves were bitten. Jackson Lynus, bitten three times in quick succession first by the initial nurse victim and then by the deranged Doctor Kozlov, fought tooth and nail, swinging his flashlight like a club until he too fell due to loss of blood.

Two Anchorage Police officers arrived just moments into the scuffle and already the situation was beginning to look grim.

There was a chaotic melee dancing and swelling like a storm cloud in the middle of the hall. To the officers it appeared that a group of deranged patients and even some staff was attacking another group of patients and staff that was trying desperately to get away. From the other side of the melee, the officers could hear screams emerging from patient rooms that had been cut off by the battle.

The tiled floor and once sterile walls were spattered with blood. The air was thick with the warm, salty smell of the fluid. Sergeant Gibson pulled his sleek semi-automatic pistol from his hip holster. With no clear targets and not sure what to do, he held the firearm aloft and fired into the ceiling, hoping to end or at least stall the fighting. It flew in the face of his training, but under the chaotic circumstances it seemed his most likely option. He hoped that the suddenness of his action, the sheer audacity of it would force everyone to stall and things could get sorted. Instead, the shot had the same effect as a starter's pistol at a race. Everyone... absolutely everyone still able to run began to sprint right at the two police officers. Sergeant Gibson and his rookie partner were hardly able to discern friend from foe. They both started to discharge their weapons at the most threatening people and faces, but their bullets didn't seem to have any effect. On more than one occasion, the 9mm slugs passed through the softer tissue of upper chests or lower abdomens, blood and sinew spraying behind, and yet the charging body scarcely showed any slackening in pace.

After each had emptied his pistol to no effect, the two officers were simply absorbed in the wave of carnage that swept over them. And the wave, like the unstoppable and inevitable tides, spilled out of the Emergency Ward and into the rest of the hospital and street outside.

7.

Neil Spencer was content with his job, but definitely not happy. He worked with a mortgage originating company in Anchorage and as such felt like he was in a position to help ordinary people realize their dreams. He was able, by getting his portion of the preliminary approval documents completed in a timely fashion, to make the oftentimes-intimidating process of becoming a first time homebuyer a little less traumatic for his "clients." He also taught classes to help people understand Alaska Housing Finance Corporation's rules and procedures; again, just trying to do more than his part. He wanted to have a job in which he wasn't merely making rich people richer and that was how it felt throughout his first seven years. He had no illusions about that now though. His ideals of making grand sweeping political and social improvements had long since faded. What was the saying—"You can be an idealist and Democrat in your twenties, but you're a fool if you weren't a capitalist and Republican by the time you were in your thirties." He wasn't to the point of being Republican yet, but he had certainly scaled down his visions for social change. He could, however, help one family at a time and make a difference in their lives. It was for that reason that he came into work early every day. Maybe he hadn't missed his chance. He found that his idealism was most prevalent early in the day, when everything still seemed possible.

And there he sat, in his office...well, his cubicle. He was thankful that it was his own cubicle and didn't have to share his rat cage with someone else like so many of his colleagues.

Small blessings could mean so much. It was just after seven in the morning, so Neil got up from his workstation and made his way to the window on the other side of the large office.

The morning rituals...his morning rituals were important to him and perhaps slightly humorous to the casual observer. He didn't drink much coffee, but having that first mug from the first pot of the day was spectacular to him. Getting to look at the whole newspaper before it had been ravaged and separated and lost was such a treat as to motivate him to be at the office well before everyone else. And of course there was the most important moment in his morning ritual.

She would get there soon. He wasn't sure of her name, though he thought he had heard her called Lani in the lobby out near the elevator. She too got to work early every day, hustled into the building, and then went upstairs to whichever company for which she worked. She dressed well but not exceptionally which led him to believe that she was perhaps an administrative assistant, accounting clerk, or human resource specialist; working some position that did most of the work and received the least of the salary and distinction.

Regardless of how she dressed, he thought she was stunning. He knew what Neil Young meant when he wished for a Cinnamon Girl. Her skin was as inviting as a sweet roll. He could only imagine how sweet she smelled. When she ran, her long curls bounced and rolled on her back and over her shoulders. She really was a thing of beauty.

Despite his attraction to her, he was still a little skittish about approaching women since his divorce. He watched every day as she backed her aged Ford Explorer into the same parking spot, checked her make-up in her rearview mirror with the colorful leis hanging from it, gathered her papers and folders from the previous night's work, and then got out. More than once, he found himself hurrying to the office door and pausing before going out into the lobby. He just couldn't bring himself to take that last but essential step. Besides, he reasoned, she was way out of his league anyway. She was beautiful and he was...well, he was him. Maybe today would be the day. Maybe he'd go out and actually strike up a conversation, introduce himself, open a door of opportunity perhaps. Maybe today he wouldn't go out into the lobby only to head directly to the Men's Room. She probably thought he had some kind of bladder condition.

He tried to shake off his doubts. He sipped his coffee, flavored with a cinnamon creamer, in nearly complete silence. There was the buzz of the office computer server, the high pitched white noise of the computers themselves, and the barely audible click of the analog wall clock hanging near the door. The quiet was nice, comforting maybe. And so he waited for her.

8.

Kurt Tolliver, getting to his office building earlier than normal, sat and waited in the comfort of his car. He was just so happy with his most recent acquisition: a green Subaru Forrester. He fidgeted with the overhead digital temperature display, clock, and compass. He was still finding new features on his car, a veritable treasure trove of gadgets and extras. The sound dampening glass very nearly muted the approaching sirens of the emergency vehicles.

He, like most people in Anchorage, was not necessarily indifferent to sirens like those unfortunate souls consigned to the life of a large American city. He was, however, distracted and in the back of his mind he remembered that they were awfully close to the hospital. The occasional siren was not completely out of the ordinary. Perhaps the sheer numbers of sirens and the feeling that they were all converging exactly where he was should have warranted some concern, but, again, he was distracted with his new car.

He got out, started to step away, and then remembered his briefcase in his back seat. He pressed the button on his door remote and, opening the rear door on the driver side, leaned into the backseat, reaching all the way across to the opposite side. The "new car" smell greeted him again like it was the first time its doors had ever been opened.

9.

Neil, standing at the window and still waiting for lovely Lani, watched as what appeared to be a drunken man staggered across the parking lot in the direction of the parked Subaru. The unsteady figure trudged through two fairly sizable water puddles in his trek across the lot. His steps were like those of a toddler but his direction was undeniable. He was on a collision course with the new green Subaru.

To Neil, the man appeared to be wearing a uniform of sorts; like a security guard perhaps. He caught faint glints of reflection from what appeared to be a badge on his chest. He thought to himself that whatever outfit he was with was certainly proud today. What a great representative for their services and their company.

He was thinking to himself that he was glad he recognized when it was time to stop drinking. He didn't envy the man's headache later today.

Neil saw the curly headed blonde guy get out of his car while the other guy got even closer.

And then Neil realized that something wasn't right. He wasn't quite sure what exactly it was. There was something exceptionally odd about the staggering man. He evinced quite a bit of agitation and maybe even aggression to Neil. As he got closer to the oblivious curly headed blonde guy, his pace quickened and his arms rose. It appeared as if he was going to grab him. And do what Neil wasn't entirely sure, but he was pretty sure that it wasn't going to be good.

10.

Kurt Tolliver, having retrieved his leather portfolio from his backseat, stood away from his car. He looked at the steel and glass building in front of him, catching sight of a reflection of a pair of sea gulls circling. Looking up and watching the birds' reflections whirl and swirl in updrafts of air, he breathed in deeply and tasted the moisture as it crawled into his lungs. Something didn't seem quite right to him, though it was just a hint of smell that tickled his nose and brought on a sneeze. As he doubled over with the force of the sneeze, he thought he heard something that sounded as if someone was hitting the inside of a window on the building.

When he had recovered from his expiation, he stood back up and saw the reflection of something else altogether in the mirrored glass in front of him. There was someone else with him; right next to him in fact. He turned and saw unbridled rage in the ravenous eyes of a man that wasn't quite human.

Kurt turned to run, but his attacker's hands found their mark; one grabbing his arm and the other finding purchase in his blonde curls. He screamed in fear, a sound that he had never heard come from himself before.

11.

Neil dropped his coffee cup and started pounding on the glass of his first floor office. But it was all for naught and too late. Like a snagged fish, Kurt Tolliver was hooked and caught.

Neil was frozen. It didn't seem that any of this could be real. How could it be? The staggering man pulled his victim to the pavement, clawing and biting and ravaging him brutally. He was acting like a wild animal, a predator who has just brought down his kill.

Neil tried in vain to move his legs but he was planted, as immobile as a granite statue. His breathing was shallow. The quiet had returned to the room, but this quiet was anything but peaceful.

Unable to think of anything else to do, he spun around and found a phone. He punched 911 on the dial pad and then walked back to his post at the window, stretching the cord behind as he went. The blonde haired guy...the victim was no longer struggling. His attacker was still violently assailing him, but, like the still very much alive moth that is devoured by the spider, the poor man was only able to flex his hands feebly, painfully with each vicious bite. Just seconds later, his hands were no longer moving. It was over. At least it should have been over, but the assailant was still biting at him and tearing away pieces of him. He was eating him.

He bit at the now exposed stomach of the man and pulled off a large piece of dripping, white flesh. He chewed hungrily and was moving in for another bite even before he'd finished the first.

That was enough for Neil. The phone, he suddenly realized, had been repeating a message about all lines being busy and to try his call back later. The voice was very sorry for any inconvenience but they were experiencing a high volume of calls right then. He just dropped the phone and ran to the storage room.

"Where the fuck is it? Where the f...?" And then he had his hands on it; a long white locking security cable for laptop computers. Looking out the window to make sure the ghoul was still busy with his fresh kill, Neil ran out to the front doors of the office building to lock them with the cable.

Getting to the door, he realized another vehicle had pulled up out front, having come in from the rear entrance. A brown Chevy truck pulled into the parking lot and parked a fair distance away from the green Subaru and the two men still on the pavement. The driver, a shortish blonde woman who Neil had seen in the building from time to time, got out and started across the lot. She was on her cell phone and completely unaware of the horror that was unfolding only yards away from her.

Neil thought to himself, who could she possibly be talking to at this hour of the morning? She got closer and closer, until she finally drew the attention of the attacker who leapt to his feet and started running toward her. She realized immediately that he was coming after her so she reeled about and ran back to her truck. She had a good lead and was able to get into the vehicle just seconds before her chaser arrived.

Neil was about to wrap the wire around the door handles when he noticed that the blond haired guy was starting to move again. In fact, the man was able to get himself to his feet again. Neil shouted, "Hey, you okay? Hey?" He was starting out the door until the man turned around and started running straight at him. As he ran, Neil watched his insides slowly spill out in red and pink folds of flesh onto the pavement and get left behind, some still attached and trailing behind him like some horrible preternatural tail.

"Fuck this!" Neil shouted as he pulled the heavy glass front doors closed. He wrapped the cable tightly around the door handles and then fastened the lock. Almost at once, the curly headed blonde guy was there clawing at the glass, leaving bloody streaks and smears. The sound he was making was anything but human. It sounded labored and primordial and hungry. Neil stood there only long enough to make sure that the woman in the truck wasn't in any immediate danger but for some reason she hadn't started the truck and driven away. The answer lay in the middle of the lot, a pile of strung black and white beads and notched metal. She'd dropped her keys in her surprise and haste and was now besieged in the very tenuous safety of her vehicle.

Neil backed away from the doors hoping that they would hold long enough for him to figure out what to do and then do it. He went back into the office and tried the phone again and only to verify that the lines were all still busy. He sat down at his chair for just a moment to think.

He wouldn't be able to get to his car because it was out front near the Subaru. He was cut off from it. He did, however, know where the keys were for the company vehicle, which was parked downstairs in a secure parking garage.

He had to think fast. He had to stay in control. What would he need? He couldn't quite control his breathing as he fought to clear his thoughts. Absently, he went to the staff refrigerator and dumped the several unopened water bottles into the bottom of an empty copy paper box. The box was a lucky find–the new janitor crew had once again, thankfully, forgotten to take all the trash when they serviced the office this weekend. He tossed into the box a partial loaf of bread and a plastic jar of peanut butter as well. He couldn't bring himself to take the leftovers in the Styrofoam containers. They just remained off limits in his mind. He grabbed the keys from the filing drawer at the front desk and even thought to grab the small set of tools on the shelf in the storeroom. The hammer he gripped in his hand and swung it several times, intending to use it more as a tomahawk or hatchet as opposed to its original purpose. He was having a hard time balancing the box, now also laden with a fire extinguisher from the wall, while trying to also hold the hammer so he elected to hook the hammer's head into a belt loop and let it hang loosely. He took three deep breaths, holding each, and tried to prepare himself to venture out. He looked at the clock as he set himself to depart, a habit he had developed over the years coming and going at the office. It was just minutes after seven in the morning.

45

He peeked out and saw the mutilated curly blonde headed man still clawing at the front doors. The security cable seemed to be holding tight, but he didn't see the point in pushing matters. Using the elevator he went down to the basement garage. The garage door was still closed tightly and the only vehicles in the garage were the company minivan, a vintage Corvette that was draped in a white dust cover, and a maintenance truck.

Neil ran as fast as his cumbersome load would allow. He all but threw himself into the front seat. Dropping the keys twice, he finally got the van started. With the doors securely locked, he sat and pondered his next move, concentrating as he did on slowing his breathing. If he wasn't careful he might hyperventilate. Calming himself, he tried to focus on the task at hand. He didn't have anything with which to defend himself and he was pretty certain that he would need something before too long. He could go to Fred Meyer's. They had food, water, and, perhaps most importantly for his peace of mind, firearms.

He opened the garage and saw another car, a small sedan, scream by nearly out of control. Even with the windows up, he could hear the wail of sirens coming from every direction. On the not too distant horizon, just in front of the sunrise still in its daily infancy, a pillar of smoke was making its lazy way to the sky. The smoke appeared to be rising up from somewhere near the hospital. He needed to get to Fred's quickly, but he didn't want to drive like that sedan. He needed to be smart. He looked at his full gas gauge and felt better. Turning on the radio though wasn't any comfort at all. He heard the test pattern and the recording that "... if this were an actual emergency...." No news.

He needed to get to the highway and head south. He needed to get to Fred Meyer's quickly before things got completely out of control. As he passed the front parking lot though, he noticed that the woman in the truck still hadn't moved. Her attacker was still pounding away at the front of the truck and on the metal doors, but thankfully he hadn't been able to breach the windows yet. Neil then saw the woman who sat up for a brief second. Even from this distance, the two of them caught one another's eyes.

Neil stopped in the middle of the road. He took a deep breath, gripped the steering wheel, and turned sharply into the parking lot. He headed straight for the truck. The woman's assailant was on the passenger side of her truck so that was where Neil aimed his van. His engine growled slightly as he fed it gas and urged it ahead quicker and quicker.

He hit the other man and sent him flying out of the parking lot and onto the grass that ran along the highway several feet away. Neil shot a look at the woman who was even then crawling out of her passenger door. Neil flipped the switch to the lock, but she was already pulling on the handle. Nothing happened. She pulled and pulled again. Neil was unable to do anything. Every time he hit the switch she was pulling. He finally reached across and flipped the lock open manually.

Screaming she hopped into the door just as the man was getting back up and over to them. Neil now saw that it was a uniform the other man was wearing. It was an apparently battle-worn security guard uniform who's name patch just above his shiny badge read: Lynus.

"You okay?"

Wild-eyed she demanded, "Just drive! Get us the fuck outta here!"

Neil swung the van around, dragging the guard Lynus through part of the parking lot until the deranged guard fell off rolling violently away. Just seconds later, Neil and his new passenger were heading north on the Seward Highway making their way toward the Midtown Fred Meyer, which was within sight of them even as they got on the main road. Neil, never taking his eyes off of the road, said, "My name is Neil."

Chuckling quietly to herself, the woman answered, "Rachel."

"Why did you laugh?"

She looked over at him and answered, "That's the name of the guy I was talking to on the phone back there."

Neil answered with a nod and nothing more. The rest of the drive was highlighted only by the repeating cycle on the radio of the Emergency Broadcast System. It was just under five minutes before they were pulling into the nearly empty parking lot of the big box store. He pulled right up to the front doors and stopped.

Rachel looked at him and asked, "What the hell are we stopping here for...some early Christmas shopping?"

"We need supplies."

"You think this is going to be some kind of fucking camping trip? We need to go to the police. We need some protection."

"Listen, I don't know if you could hear or not, but I think I heard every siren in the city heading toward the hospital. My guess is that there aren't any police left to help us. And until they can, we've got to help ourselves. There is something really weird and really wrong going on right now and what I'd like to do is get out of its way."

"What'd' you have in mind?"

"First things first, I'm Neil," and he offered his hand in the way of a formal introduction.

12.

Authorities in bunkered hospital offices tried desperately to determine what was happening and what could be done about it. They watched on surveillance cameras as groups of fleeing survivors moved from floor to floor and from department to department. There seemed to be no exits still available. There was also no time to talk and to plan as each door or stairwell that was barricaded was systematically broken down and through which hordes of attackers poured. And as each new area was abandoned, fewer and fewer members of these groups continued. They were being exterminated little by little.

In one group, Dr. Caldwell who had been trying to treat little Martin Houser much earlier that morning, was starting to understand that any bite regardless of severity or treatment was lethal. Even more troubling was that he was also beginning to understand that the bites also initiated a biological change in the victim that ultimately led to ...the reanimation of dead tissue. It was all but impossible for him to accept. He was a man of science and healing and this was the stuff of science fiction.

The reanimated victims were only human in appearance, retaining no memory, no faculties aside from basic ambulation and senses, and no restraint or fear. What they did develop, however, was a seemingly insatiable hunger and a ruthless disregard for any sense of compassion. They became, in essence, cannibalistic homicidal machines.

The horrific things he had seen today made his head swim and his stomach turn. Patients, restricted to their beds by injury or illness, were butchered where they lay. Recovery rooms had become hellish smorgasbords. He shuddered to think what had happened to those innocents in the nursery and in the NICU. Maybe the monsters hadn't made it that far yet. Maybe the security doors had been blocked and had held the mob at bay.

He looked at what remained of their group. There were maybe twenty people with him. They were exhausted and terrified and not sure where they were going to go next. He wasn't sure on what floor they were, but knew that they couldn't keep going up indefinitely. Eventually they'd come to the top floor and be trapped. If only they could know where to go or what to do, but even then he could hear the moaning from the stairwell getting louder and closer. They were still being followed. He knew they had to keep moving, but before they did he wanted to do a quick assessment of their group.

There was one police officer with them, though his pistol had proven largely ineffective in even slowing the pursuers let alone discouraging or stopping the pursuit. There were a couple of maintenance workers in long blue coveralls, some nurses (both male and female), and a collection of administrative personnel such as office clerks and secretaries. Perhaps most troubling, especially if his hypothesis about the effects of the bites was true, there were three members of the group who had been bitten and one of them was starting to look more and more like that little boy from whom all of this had started.

He took the police officer aside to express his fears. The officer nodded as he listened but his face twisted in incredulity. He listened to everything the doctor had to say and then asked, "So what are you saying Doc? Should we leave those three here or just shoot them now?" There was a certain degree of skepticism in the officer's words but enough seriousness to indicate that the officer was at least aware that these were very serious options that needed to be considered.

Just then, the two of them heard a phone ring in an open office to their right. It rang three times and then stopped. Then it rang another three times and stopped. As it began to ring again, Dr. Caldwell picked it up and cautiously answered, "Hello?"

"Doctor," a voice began, "I need you to head to the top floor. Do everything you can to block any and all doors. We're going to get you out of there, but you have to put some space between you and them. Do you understand?"

"Yes, but how do you..."

"We've been keeping an eye on you with the security cameras. Your trackers are about two floors down from you but headed your way. We need you to get moving now. Get upstairs as fast as you can, but remember to block the stairs and any doors as well as you can. Do any of the maintenance men with you have their keys on them? Can they lock the doors?"

"No. Their keys don't work in this tower but we'll do our best."

"Doctor, I don't want to hear that you'll do your best. We need you to take charge and get those people out of there. Do you understand me?"

"Yessir."

"Okay, if you get to other phones and need help, call me back at extension 1138."

"Thanks, but who is this?"

"My name is Simon."

13.

Owen Hollander, battalion commander for the Anchorage Fire Department, was only vaguely aware of the scale of the chaos in the hospital area. He was acutely aware, however, that Providence Hospital, one of the most important emergency response centers in the city, was burning. The lack of any firm communication from the area caused him even more concern. While he had heard of looting and some possible homicides being committed, he was relatively certain that even looters and murderers would allow a fire engine to pass. Even at their worst, most people recognized the value and benefit of a functioning hospital and would not interfere with firemen trying to do their jobs.

So, with that in mind, he ordered two engine companies of firefighters to report to the hospital with a third to stand in ready reserve. These men were dispatched within minutes of the tumult's beginning at the hospital. Unfortunately, due to some unforeseen atmospheric interference, he had lost contact with his men shortly after their arrival at the scene. After several attempts using a wide range of tools to re-establish a communication link, he had decided that he and the third engine company would wade into the fray to lend their support to their comrades already engaged.

He climbed into his red sport utility vehicle that served as his command vehicle and led the way. As they got nearer, he saw more and more people running from the scene. It must be worse than he originally thought. There were abandoned police cars on either side of the road and other vehicles scattered here and there, some still in the road and with engines idling. The sun was still coming up, so he was unsure what the objects were that were lying about, though they seemed eerily similar to bodies. He was suddenly worried that perhaps there had been a chemical spill of some sort that was posing a respiration hazard. He called back on his radio to the engine following him and voiced his concerns about possible toxic fumes in the air. He and the company chief decided that they needed to press on and to observe the strictest caution in their approach.

They were soon on Providence Drive and only a handful of blocks from the hospital. It was here that things really began to sour. Owen could see the pulsing lights of one of his engines in the distance. It didn't appear as if it had actually made it to the hospital. He tried to reach his silent teams with his radio and then with his cell phone. Nothing. He was going into the emergency scene completely blind as to what to expect. It was troubling, but then again he was a firefighter and, as such, was expected to think on his feet and use his better judgment in just such scenarios.

He pressed his accelerator and sped ahead of the more cumbersome fire engine. If he could get a better idea of the nature of the emergency, he might be able to better prepare his men for what to expect. He wasn't quite sure what to anticipate himself, but for what he saw there was no anticipating.

One of his dispatched fire engines was just around the bend in the road and just short of the hospital. It was sitting slightly off the road with its lights still flashing. The eerie thing about it was that there was no one around it. Not a single one of his men could be seen. There were helmets and some other emergency gear scattered around, but no firefighters. He called again on his radio. Still nothing. He slowed his vehicle to get a better look. He lowered his window and called on his radio again. Even from there he could hear his voice come from the radio in the open cab of the large emergency vehicle.

Then he saw a body lying on the side of the road. It was lying face down but was wearing a firefighter's heavy coat. He slammed on his breaks and leapt from his truck. Instinctively, he put on his helmet and ran across the road to the fallen fireman. Owen ran through his training and followed the proper routine for approaching a potentially injured person in an emergency setting.

He called as he neared him, "Can you hear me? I'm here to help. Are you okay?"

There was no response. He picked up his pace and was all but next to the man when he noticed some movement. A group of screaming, fleeing people caught his eye and distracted him for a moment. He looked back down and the man was slowly lifting himself up onto all fours. Owen leaned down and got an arm under his fallen comrade to help hoist him up onto his feet. His hand was immediately wet and sticky. He withdrew it involuntarily and was disgusted to see that it was covered in blood...rich, bright red blood. He almost fell backward.

When the firefighter was fully on his feet but still not facing him, Owen asked cautiously, "Are you okay?"

The stricken man spun around and grabbed hold of the Battalion Chief, sinking his teeth into his cheek. Owen kicked the other man hard in the leg, knocking him off balance enough to get away. He turned to escape, but ran headlong into another person, a woman, whose left side of her face was mutilated. Her eye socket was ripped open horribly and her eye was gone. Her outer ear too was missing and huge swaths of skin from her neck had been shorn away by something. Owen tried to speak, but she was on him before a single word could be uttered. The firefighter still behind him was also grabbing at him as the two pulled him from his feet.

His radio was squawking desperately as the fire engine following him arrived on the scene.

14.

After their official if brief introductions, Neil and Rachel formulated a plan, deciding what was absolutely necessary should their time be cut short. She was going to get a cart and head toward the canned foods, the bottled water, granola bars, and anything else that required the least amount of preparation. He headed for the Sports Department to look at the guns and camping gear.

The Sports Department was more or less in the middle of the store. Even without the signs pointing him that way, he could have found it by moving toward the fishing poles whose long necks peered up and over the tops of the tall shelving units that delineated shopping aisles. In the midst of the department sat a locked glass cabinet, behind which stood a bank of carefully displayed rifles and shotguns. He had never owned a firearm before, but was not intimidated by them either. He realized, however, that he wasn't entirely sure what to get. He climbed over the counter and was immediately overwhelmed with the varieties. He knew that he wanted at least one hunting rifle with a scope, maybe a couple of shotguns, and at least one smaller rifle. The glass cabinet holding the handguns was also of interest to him. He wanted to have everything that they might need. Deciding on the handguns first, he retrieved a fire extinguisher from a support column and smashed the top of the cabinet. He just started grabbing everything onto which he could lay his hands. He grabbed heavy revolvers and lighter, sleeker automatics. There were some laser sights and other accessories in the bottom, but he elected not to get these. He then moved his shopping cart over to the wall behind and by the armloads started to empty the shelves of ammunition. He grabbed everything; not a bit was left. On top of all of this he piled several rifles, more rifles than he had originally intended. Of course, all of the firearms had locked security bolts essentially freezing their triggers. Seeing this but deciding to move on and deal with it later, Neil next went to the camping section.

From these aisles, Neil put his hands on sleeping bags, hooking them to the outside of the cart. He was just about to pile in a small tent when a voice behind him made him jump.

"What the hell are you doing?"

He turned to see the woman whose voice hard startled him. It was the manager...or at least a manager of the store. She seemed too young to be the general manager, but her nametag, which read "Meghan", also boasted that she was "Management." She glared at him with her intense blue eyes and demanded a response.

Neil was embarrassed during the brief silence that ensued. Looking down at the shopping cart and at the potential arsenal in it, he was at a loss for words to explain his actions. He was finding it hard to immediately explain to her why he was doing what he was doing. He wasn't quite sure how many laws he had broken but he was relatively certain that it was more than he could imagine. It just wasn't in his nature to break the law and yet he hadn't even hesitated to...steal and vandalize.

More annoyed than anything else the woman asked, "What the hell is going on today? Has everyone gone crazy?"

Stuttering, Neil tried, "I...um...I..."

"I mean, first no one shows up for work this morning... last time I'm hiring college students that live on campus. I mean, you'd think as close as it was it would be a snap to get here for work. And then you...Are you looting?"

"No," of this Neil was adamant. Looting just seemed too random and self-serving. What he had done was self-preserving. "Have you turned on a radio this morning? Watched the news? Anything?"

Thoughtfully, she answered, "Uhhh, no. My radio is on the blink in my car and the music in here is a recording."

Knowing that this would be the quickest way to get his

point across, Neil suggested, "Why don't you go call the police. I'll come with you."

They went to the front of the store to use the phone at the Customer Service Desk. Meghan was careful to go inside the enclosure and leave Neil standing on the store sales floor. In case he was off the deep end, she wanted to have something between her and him, even if it was only the pressboard walls of the customer service island. After she dialed and heard the same recording Neil had heard earlier, she dialed her home number; same recording. She took her cell phone from her pocket and tried that as well only to get the same frustrating message.

Neil said, "Let's go over to the Electronics section and check out the news. Maybe someone is still broadcasting." Test patterns were on every television from every station; a simple message ran along the bottom that a word from the Emergency Broadcast System would follow shortly.

Meghan asked again as she accompanied Neil out to his van which was parked just outside the doors, "What's going on?"

Seriously, almost apologetically, Neil looked her squarely in the eyes and said, "I don't honestly know for sure. I just saw the most disturbing and frightening thing I think I could ever imagine."

And so, as they finished unloading the supplies he had gathered into the rear hatch and back seat of his van and then went back into the store to load the cart with other necessities such as matches and fire starting bricks, batteries, first aid supplies, and anything else they thought might be useful, he told her about what had happened to Rachel and him at their office building. Neil avoided any speculation or editorializing about the events; there really wasn't any point. The facts themselves were staggering enough without side comments.

Perhaps it was because of the way that Neil had talked about it, but Meghan felt compelled to believe the story. When she saw Rachel pass by with a cart so full she could barely push it, she knew they were telling the truth. There was something that still clung to Rachel's face and eyes. A sense of fear and doubt just seemed to cling to the other woman.

They were startled when a new voice shouted from the front of the store, "Helllllloooooo! Is there anyone herrrreee? Can anyone help us?"

Neil and Meghan pushed their full cart out to the voice, which happened to be on the way to the van parked out front. It was a younger man, not much more than a kid really, who waited for them by the Customer Service Desk. He had two young children who looked wild-eyed and scared with him.

15.

And so Jerry recounted to the others what had happened at the hospital, allowing Danny and Jules to fill in details of how it all began with poor little Martin and their caveman.

"...so, we got out to my car in the parking garage and then there was all this screaming and running all around us. There were people running every which way. Some were chasin' and some were fleein.' We were already in our car and moving, so we were able to get the hell outta Dodge before it was too late. There weren't a whole lot of others who were that lucky though. A bus pulled up just as we got out onto Providence Drive. I don't think the driver could see what was going on 'cause he just opened his doors and waited. Like everything was still normal and he was just going to pick up his passengers like any other day. Those things were on there before he could do anything. I think I saw the bus start moving again, but we just wanted to get away fast."

Jules pulled on Jerry's blue paper thin "scrub" pants and asked him but loud enough for everyone to hear clearly, "What about my Mom and Dad? Where are they? Are they going to be alright?"

Jerry couldn't look down at her. He just couldn't bring himself to do that. He knew their probable fate. They had been there at the epicenter of all of the chaos. He touched her lightly on her head. He swallowed hard and instead looked at the other adults.

The question hung in the air though for all of the adults gathering around to hear, Rachel had by then joined them. Meghan was still not sure what was happening. Neil and Rachel had seen an attack and were not sure of what they had actually seen other than a very grisly and bizarre murder. Jerry was the only one among them who understood and even he wasn't entirely able to wrap his mind around the truth.

The air was heavy with unease and doubt. They looked at one another for a brief few moments unsure of what to do. Neil interrupted the silence with, "Okay. Unless there are any objections, I think we should try and sort things out somewhere other than here. Does anyone live close by?"

Rachel protested with a loud, "Fuck that! Oh, sorry kids."

"D'you have a different idea?"

"Everything we need is right here. Why don't we just stay here and wait for..." She trailed off realizing that she didn't know how to finish her thought.

Neil finished it for her. "Wait here for what? We're on our own here. This is why I think we should get out of here and, by the way; the clock on that train is ticking away so I'll make this brief. This place has too many windows that can be broken and too many lights to draw attention to itself. This place is bad news."

Jerry added, "He's right...Rachel is it? This place would be a deathtrap. We need to go somewhere that won't attract a lot of people; because where there are lots of people there will be lots of those things. It's that simple."

Meghan summed up the decision with, "Okay. Then let's get moving. If I'm gonna die, I don't want it to be at work."

Her candor and dry humor brought a smile to everyone's face as they went back to the parking lot and their awaiting all-wheel drive life raft.

When they stepped outside, the sky was getting brighter, the smoke coming from near the hospital appeared to be getting thicker and broader as if the base of the flames was starting to devour the college campus as well as the hospital, but the most unsettling thing was the almost totally absent sound of emergency sirens. Not more than fifteen minutes prior, the air was filled with the clarion echoes of police cars, ambulances, and fire trucks. Now the only thing in the air was the smell of smoke as the city started to burn.

And then there was something else: a hum really. Jerry had

once been to a horse race and it sounded strangely similar to that. He said uneasily, "I think we'd just better get outta here."

Rachel asked, "What is that sound," and stepped away from the van trying to see around the corner toward the source of the approaching sound. It grew louder and louder until they could make out what was undoubtedly screams.

The chaos had found them and was moving very quickly toward them. They had to act immediately.

Meghan fished her keys from her pocket and ran toward her car. Neil shouted after her, "What the hell are you doing?"

"I'm not leaving my car here. I'll follow you."

She stopped suddenly and ran back to him. "Here," she said, handing him a fistful of keys. "This one should unlock the trigger guards on the guns."

Neil smiled and said, "Thanks and here," passing one of the two-way radios he had grabbed from the Electronics Department. "Stay in contact with us. I don't want to lose you."

She smiled and ran over to her car, which took several attempts to start. She then bolted over to the Tesoro gas station in the northwest corner of the parking lot. Neil, Jerry, Rachel, and the two kids all loaded themselves into Neil's minivan and followed Meghan to the service station.

Neil was surprised when he got there to find that she wasn't getting gas. She was corralling two other people, employees at the gas station, into her car. As he pulled up next to her, she gave him the thumbs up, rolled down her window, and asked, "Okay, so now what?

He wasn't entirely sure what was next. They could get on the Glenn Highway and head north out of town. They could get on the Seward Highway and head south out of town. As far as getting out of town, those were the only two options. Neil was concerned that if this chaos, like ripples in a pond from a dropped stone, was spreading in every direction, that the highway north might be too snarled with outgoing traffic. He really didn't relish the thought of getting stuck in a traffic jam and then having to beat this storm on foot. The southbound highway was a little more appealing, but once they headed south they were very limited with any other road travel. Of course, they could just find a good place to hide and wait. But where?

16.

The chaos at Providence Hospital had, by that time, grown exponentially. The University of Alaska Anchorage, immediately adjacent to the hospital, was engulfed by the terrifying wave as it spread further and further into the city. Like a metastasizing cancer, the bedlam sought fertile grounds of hapless victims in the neighborhoods and schools surrounding the university and hospital. The city was still rousing itself from its slumber, so any response by the citizenry was limited at best.

Young children waiting for the school bus to pick them up for school, men and women out for their morning exercise jogs or walks, and clueless souls retrieving their morning newspapers were the first victims to fall. Entire neighborhoods were shaken awake by the horrible cries and desperate pleas for help from the latest victims.

One woman watched from her bay window as a group of four or five of the fiends ran down the street chasing after her newspaper deliveryman. Not realizing what was happening, she flew to her front door and started to scream at his pursuers just as they overcame his flight. While two of them pinned him down and started to perform their awful work, the others altered their course and ran at her. She slammed her door heavily behind her just as they were topping the stairs of her front porch. Locking it, she screamed and ran for the phone. In the living room of her condominium, she was able to punch in 9-1-1 just as one of her attackers plunged through her bay window and was upon her. She kicked and screamed but it was no use. She was dragged to the floor as she tried to run and suffered the same fate as every other victim. Slowly the neighborhood and every other neighborhood bordering the university and hospital area were awakened by screams of terror as the disease, bit by bit, slowly consumed the city.

17.

D r. Caldwell and his group, now down to just eight people, were trying to catch their breath on a floor dominated by small labs and private physicians' offices. He and the police officer had not acted upon his suspicions of the effects of the bites and had, instead, elected to move the three members of their group who had been injured thus. The doctor was always certain to isolate the three away from the rest of the group. No point in taking any chances. He could be wrong but if he was right, he didn't want to invite disaster. Two floors later, the person who appeared to have the worst bites and who was in rapid decline expired and almost immediately reanimated.

The living corpse, still lying between the two other bitten people, leaned across one of the injured people's laps and started to chew on her thigh, which was showing just below her skirt. Even through her disorienting misery, the victim tried to fend off her attacker. She hit the other woman on the back of the head until she had somewhat relented. Of course, she merely stopped biting her victim on the leg and moved her blood slathered teeth and lips up to her neck.

The third wounded person, a diminutive Filipino man, tried to crawl away using his one good arm to balance himself. He was unable to make any headway though as he succumbed to his dizziness and collapsed onto his stomach. He mercifully passed out and was still unconscious as the two others, the second woman having died from her new wounds and reanimated, started to chew on his legs and arms.

Soon, the three of them were sitting in a thick and growing pool of red that coursed out on the tiled floor and found its way under the door and into the hall.

Officer Ivanoff, the Anchorage policeman in Dr. Caldwell's group, was dispatched to retrieve the three wounded people who had been stashed away in a removed office. When he rounded a corner, he immediately saw the blood on the floor. He stopped and stood motionless and quiet. The door to the office was still shut and anything leaving the room would have to pass through the crimson puddle and would thus be forced to leave footprints wherever it trod. There was absolutely no evidence of anyone or anything having left the office. He stood there for a moment or two not sure of what to do. He did, however, instinctively remove his pistol from its holster.

He couldn't bring himself to just leave without at least verifying his and the doctor's suspicions, so he asked tentatively, "How we doin' in there? Anyone awake?"

He started to step forward but jumped back, his eyes wide with shock, when the face appeared in the window of the office door. It was the woman in the short skirt. Her once smooth, dark skin was faded almost gray except around her eyes which were darker than her skin had been before. Her hungry eyes looked into the hallway and caught sight of Officer Ivanoff. From behind the door, he could hear her deep, chesty grunting and moaning that resonated with a primal hunger that turned the police officer's stomach. It was the first time he had ever felt like prey. It was a feeling that sapped all of his strength.

The grey-skinned woman started to press herself against the door, trying to get at her quarry. He couldn't move. He was revolted and terrified and utterly paralyzed. She leaned into the door harder and harder, pressing her face against the glass and streaking it with the blood that had spurted from the open wounds on her neck onto her cheeks.

Dr. Caldwell was then at his side, having responded to the sounds he was hearing. He was standing to the side and slightly behind the police officer when he saw the woman behind the glass. He stood there and watched.

Officer Ivanoff asked, never taking his eyes off of her, "Did you lock that door Doc?"

"No. I'm guessing you didn't either."

"Nope."

"Maybe that's a good thing. One good piece of news."

"And what's that?"

The doctor nodded his head and thought aloud, "Perhaps these things are not able to even retain the simplest of motor functions. Opening a door with a turning door handle may actually be beyond them."

"Well, how have they been getting through all the doors all day long then?"

"My guess is that..."

"Your guess? Your guess? What do you mean, 'your guess'?"

"You act like I'm an authority here on this. Until a little while ago, I would have said that all of this was an impossibility that only could happen in science fiction. Again, my guess is that the other doors were opened by sheer weight of numbers. When the door is actually pushed from its frame, it doesn't matter whether they can use door knobs or not...they're comin' through."

Out of frustration over not being able to get through, the woman finally smashed her head through the glass of the small window on the door. Still unable to pass through, the only immediate result was that now one of her arms was extending into the hallway and her moaning was that much louder.

Her moaning solo soon became a trio as the other two recently expired souls joined her. Dr. Caldwell, shaking his head, unnecessarily uttered, "We'd better get going again. It won't take long for the three of them to force that door open and the others can't be that much farther behind us now."

"Yeah. I know. Ya know that pretty soon we're gonna run outta places to run to. We only got so many floors before we get to the top."

"I know officer."

"Well, what are we gonna do when we get to the top?"

"I don't know yet. I'm hoping that Simon has the answers."

And with that, a phone in an open office next to them started to ring.

18.

Neil and the group with him were traveling west on Northern Lights Boulevard. That was really the only option left to them after they finally exited the Fred Meyer and Tesoro parking lots. The maelstrom had all but caught up with them and was actually starting to envelope their north and southbound escape routes.

Neil just kept thinking to himself, just keep moving...get away. It didn't matter to where. All that mattered was getting there.

Jules looked over the back seat through a crack in the piles of looted supplies. She didn't know what she was looking at or why she was looking anymore. All she knew was that somewhere back there was her family. All of these strange grownups were acting scared and really nervous and that made her scared and really nervous. It was frustrating though because she wasn't certain why she was made to feel scared and nervous. Events had unfolded so quickly that she hadn't really been able to keep pace. All that she could really remember was that her brother was sick and her mom and dad were trying to get him better. If Danny wasn't with her, she doubted that she could be there either. She would have been too scared to go with these strangers, even though they seemed like kind people that only wanted to protect her. She trusted Danny though.

And Danny. He wasn't quite sure what he was feeling. He was terrified of the possibilities and yet... Inside every adolescent boy is a hero myth waiting to play itself out. The hero rising above catastrophe to triumph and everything always worked out for the best. Sometimes the hero died but usually he found a way out. That was how the movies were. That was how video games were.

He wasn't in any hurry to start volunteering to fight, but then again the best heroes were always the reluctant champions. He would watch the grownups with the guns and learn how they work. Maybe he could stick close to Neil. He seemed smart and actually knew what was going on. He got all this stuff in the back of the van and then put them on the road. Danny hoped that they were on a road out of town but just to be moving felt good.

Unfortunately, there were only two roads that led out of Anchorage: the Glenn Highway that headed north toward the Matanuska-Susitna Valley and the Seward Highway that headed south toward the Kenai Peninsula. They were on neither but they were headed in exactly the opposite direction from which the noise and commotion had come. Danny knew none of the information about the roads. He was keenly aware of the last point and was very grateful for that decision by Neil.

19.

Dr. Caldwell was one floor from the roof but had his hands full with getting there. They were all but ambushed at the main exit to the roof and were forced to retreat deep into some administrative offices. Unfortunately, most of the doors behind them were glass.

A phone rang on a desk next to the doctor. Everyone jumped and held their breath. He answered it as they all released a forced chuckle of a sigh.

"Hello Simon."

"I don't have much time and neither do you. Above your heads is a heating duct. If you spread yourselves out enough, it should withstand your weight. Head north in the duct and find an access panel on your right about a hundred feet in. Go through it, climb the ladder and you'll be on the roof. Transportation will be there shortly. You've got the last ride outta here doctor."

"Will we see you there Simon?"

"No, I'm afraid I am trapped in the control room and it's just a matter of time. Nowhere to go you know. Glad I could help."

And the line went dead.

"Okay, Simon says we got a way out above our heads. Up through the ceiling and into the duct. I guess I should go first since I know where we're goin.' Let's get movin' right away. He said we haven't got much time."

Simon was right. Officer Ivanoff was the last up into the duct. He reached back with his foot and kicked away the chair they had used as a boost. Hanging precariously, he saw entire walls of glass come down as their hunters tracked them relentlessly. The sound was terrific and shook the duct beneath them.

The doctor found the access panel and was soon on the roof, but there was nothing there. No magic carpet to ferry them away from danger. How long did they have he wondered. He looked over the side of the tower to the ground below. It wasn't the tallest building in Anchorage, but it was tall enough to know that it was suicide to jump. Besides, the bedlam below was staggering. It was a scene right out of hell. Neither Milton nor Dante could have imagined a more vivid depiction of absolute terror. And he was about to become a part of it.

He vomited over the edge. He leaned into the railing and wretched the early morning breakfast he'd eaten. Chunks of moist bagel with a broth of Earl Grey Tea sprayed out of his mouth, burning his nose and back of his throat as it exited. He was pretty sure that he was crying but it didn't even really matter anymore.

He stood himself up straight and wiped his face clean with his once-white lab coat. He turned and looked at his party of followers. "I'm sorry. There's nowhere left to run. Maybe Simon's chariot already left town without us," his words, voice, and demeanor were all swollen and heavy with regret.

The door for roof access, not far from where they all stood, was suddenly jarred from the inside. One of the maintenance men, Nestor, said approvingly, "Those doors are locked. Maybe they'll get bored or forget about us or something. Maybe they'll just wander away."

Officer Ivanoff bit his lower lip and counted the bullets he had remaining. It wasn't good news. They were all but defenseless and trapped. And then shots rang out from another rooftop on the opposite side of the hospital. And there, sitting gracefully and eager was the red, white, and blue Air Evacuation Helicopter. The rotors were already starting to turn as the beautiful bird came to life. The shooter, an apparent crewman was running across the heli-pad and threw himself into the open side door just as the chopper was lifting itself into the air. Hot on the heels of the liftoff was a crowd of the monsters, several of which hurled themselves over the edge of the tower as they vainly tried to follow the helicopter.

To everyone's relief, the helicopter abruptly turned and

nosed itself toward them. It was an excruciating moment before the aircraft was hovering just above them. The pilot lowered the craft slowly and then stopped just short of the surface.

Dr. Caldwell rightly surmised that the pilot was not touching all the way down. He and Ivanoff helped lift one after the other of their surviving number up into the doorway. Doctor Caldwell was the last to be hoisted onto the helicopter, so he was closest to the still open door as they motored away. From this vantage point, he could truly appreciate the gravity of the situation from which they had been removed.

The carnage that he had been able to see while they were still on the tower was merely the tip of the virtual iceberg. The UAA Bookstore was smoldering and its parking lot, recently refinished and black, was littered with corpses; dozens of bodies, some of which were moving, were lying twisted and contorted amongst the bright yellow stripes. Dr. Caldwell knew full well that the moving bodies weren't survivors or merely wounded. They would soon join the ranks of the ghouls that were streaming down Providence Drive below.

Early morning motorists that chose to listen to self-help tapes, sales training demos, or music compact discs instead of the radio drove tragically unaware that they were headed straight into the open mouth of hell. The doctor shook his head in disbelief.

The pilot motioned to his headset and then pointed to another hanging on the firewall behind him. The doctor connected the cords as he had done in helicopters in Iraq and gave a thumbs-up signal.

The pilot said, "Simon said good luck."

"And Simon?"

"I was on with him when those things got through the door. It didn't sound pretty."

Doctor Caldwell chewed the inside of his cheek and nodded.

"Hey Doc, I got some more not so good news."

"Yeah?"

"I got about enough fuel with this many people aboard to get us airborne long enough to find another spot to land. I'm guessing Merrill Field is a mess already or soon will be so I'm not heading us that way."

Doctor Caldwell suggested, "What about out toward Kincaid? Kulis is out that way and we got Anchorage International between there and here."

"Yeah, but that ain't necessarily a good thing Doc. It could get kinda dicey through there if people are in a hurry gettin' outta town, ya know."

"Got any better ideas?"

"We're on it. One more thing Doc. Can you help out Stan here? I think he may have had a closer call than he wanted."

"What happened?"

Stan, in the co-pilot seat, looked back and showed Dr. Caldwell the bite wound on his right hand. His flight suit's sleeve was already saturated with blood that was flowing heavily out of the swollen tear in the skin and muscle tissue in the fleshy part of his hand between the thumb and index finger.

Dr. Caldwell held his breath and did his best to not betray his feelings and said, "I'll do my best," and smiled.

II

20.

Whhen the radio suddenly began to speak, everyone in Neil's van was caught off guard. It had been silent for so long Neil had forgotten that he had left it on.

"...Emergency Information Broadcast to follow..."

A series of familiar beeps and tones then filled the expectant silence as they waited for news...any news.

Another voice, this one sounding more human and less recorded than the previous, began, "Attention Anchorage. This message is being broadcast from the newly established National Guard checkpoint at the Knik Bridge. A dire state of emergency has been declared for Anchorage and the rest of Southcentral Alaska.

"Reports of widespread destruction of public and private property and potential homicides are true. It is recommended that all residents remain at home. Lock all doors and stay clear of windows. Do not, I repeat, do not attempt to evacuate. Escape routes north and south are currently blocked. If you are already on either the Glenn or Seward Highways, please lock your doors and remain in your cars. Authorities will come to you and escort you safely out.

"The Governor has mobilized the Alaska State National Guard to try and contain the disturbance. At this point, authorities are unsure of the identities of the perpetrators, their resources, or their intentions. Anyone with any information about this group or their leaders is encouraged to contact authorities immediately. The Federal Bureau of Investigation and the Department of

Homeland Security have been asked to share assistance in bringing this disturbance to a quick close. Security personnel have also been dispatched to secure the Trans-Alaska Pipeline against any potential threats."

Neil said quietly, "They think this is a bunch of terrorists with some kind of political agenda. They haven't got a clue. Do they?"

The voice continued, "If you feel that your safety is at all compromised, a list of safe emergency collection sites will follow. If you are able, remain at home and wait for the authorities to resolve this situation. We will continue to broadcast developments as they are reported."

More instructions, some speculation, and lists of potential safe sites followed. Neil looked in the rearview mirror and caught Jerry's eyes. "They don't know what's happening, do they?"

"No."

"Jesus."

"And if they don't figure it out sooner rather than later, this thing will get completely outta control."

"And then?"

Jerry remembered one of the only lines he could recall from a World Literature class he took, "Abandon all hope."

Rachel, in the passenger seat, shifted her weight in the chair so that she could turn and more or less face Neil and Jerry. "If they don't figure it out...They? What about us? We're in the middle of it and I don't have a clue as to what's going on. Will somebody please tell me! And why the hell aren't we going to one of those safe sites?"

Reluctantly, Jerry answered, "Those safe sites will act like magnets for those things. They'll be drawn to the noise, the movement and the smells. We'll be safer if we just keep moving."

Still not quite sure what to think or even believe, Rachel nodded her head for lack of any better gesture that she could imagine. She checked her cell phone again and was told once again that all circuits were busy and to please try her call again later. She hoped that her boyfriend was safe. He was a firefighter assigned to Station Four on Tudor Road. If she could just speak with him, she might be able to calm down at least a little bit. His voice and his demeanor usually had a calming effect on her. She needed that right now. She needed to feel safe.

Jules and Danny grew tired of all the grownup talk. They looked out the side windows at all the businesses and then houses they passed. Jules looked over at her companion and asked, "What happened to my mom and dad? Where is Martin? When will we be back with them? Are we still going to be home in time to start school or do you think we might be able to miss a few days?"

Danny said without moving his eyes, "I think you might be getting an extended summer vacation Jules."

"Well I guess that's alright then. I was going to be in Mrs. Dumont's class and I hear she's mean."

Neil led them from Northern Lights Boulevard and turned south on Minnesota Drive, a wide major thoroughfare that connected downtown Anchorage and South Anchorage. His intention was to take Minnesota to South Anchorage and then continue further south on the Old Seward Highway as far as he was able before getting onto the New Seward Highway.

They began to pass motorists who were still going on with their normal routines, oblivious to the calamity that was unfolding. Neil flashed his headlights at cars that sped in the opposite direction as him, but his efforts went largely unnoticed. The only responses he did get were bewildered stares, waving smiles, and obscene hand gestures.

Minnesota Drive started its trek out of downtown Anchorage heading south, but, upon reaching the south side, it abruptly changed course toward the east. The uninterrupted highway drive ended at the intersection with the Old Seward Highway. They came to that traffic light and waited for just a second as Neil assessed the possibility of getting on the New Seward Highway and hightailing it out of town. In front of them, they could see the overpass where the New Seward Highway crossed over Minnesota. There were cars, largely motionless, lined up bumper to bumper for as far as they were able to see. Neil was suddenly concerned that he'd made a fatal error in judgment. Maybe they should have headed north instead. Maybe they could have gotten on the Glenn Highway ahead of the majority of the cars that now were blocking it.

Just as they turned right onto the Old Seward Highway

and continued their trek south, Jerry noticed that, like a snowball growing exponentially as it rolled down hill, a surge of drivers and passengers abandoned their vehicles and started to run. Jerry touched Neil's shoulder and pointed to the commotion.

They watched for just a heartbeat. Like spooked cattle, they stampeded south along the elevated highway. Some along the outside of the lanes were forced over the guard railing on the overpass and others simply jumped for lack of any better options. Of course, not far behind were the predators that were tracking them. The sound of horns was replaced by shrieks of terror. The din rose until it became a single, desperate scream.

They didn't need to see anymore, but Meghan, who had only been told what was happening and hadn't actually witnessed any of it, paused her car briefly. She was speechless. It resembled the images she had seen on CNN of the Running of the Bulls in Pamplona, Spain.

One man, carrying a small child, started to climb over the railing to flee down the grassy slope. He got one leg over and then was jolted back from something behind him. He pulled himself forward and then, to everyone's astonishment, threw the child, who couldn't have been more than three years old. The child hit the grassy incline and rolled down, looking like a ball of flailing legs and arms. Meghan started to pull her car out of its turn to go retrieve the child, but stopped herself when she saw three others leap over the railing and follow the child. The three following didn't appear to be doing so out of concern. Their body language spoke much more like hunters than rescuers. She couldn't bring herself to watch anymore. All she felt was disgust with herself for having done nothing. She turned her car south, rejoined Neil in his flight, and refused to look back again, even when they entered a mixed residential and commercial section of road that completely obscured the highway from view.

It was in this area that she heard and then felt the first sputter from her car's engine. She knew immediately that her car and its failing fuel pump were choosing today to challenge her patience. Her boyfriend, actually her fiancée but they had been engaged for so long that she doubted they'd ever be married, promised several times to fix it for her; but like his promise of marriage, this one had gone no further than just words. She felt herself getting angry with him and even imagined the argument and the excuses. She caught herself in her imaginings though and was overcome with concern for him all at once. For all his faults, and he had a few, he was a genuinely good guy to her and didn't actually intend to let her down.

He was the night manager of the Tesoro 2Go Mart on Tudor; down near the native hospital...not that far off from where all this had reportedly started. Was he all right? She hated to cry in front of people, especially people that she only knew in passing, so she swallowed her grief and her tears for later.

The two she picked up from the Tesoro were Tony and Kim, cashiers that she saw on most mornings when she stopped in for her morning "gas station coffee." There was just something about coffee gotten from a gas station that she craved. She had opined in the past that gas station coffee makers were secretly lacing their brew with heroin or at least some kind of hyper-caffeine that she just couldn't resist.

Both Tony and Kim learned to anticipate her arrival when it was her turn to open the big retail store with which their small station shared a parking lot. They just timed the coffee making around her schedule. At least, that was how it appeared to her and she appreciated that.

That was, however, the extent to which she knew them. She didn't even know their last names and there she was on the verge of tears in front of them. She fought them back for control. And then she felt the hand fall softly on her shoulder. It was Tony, sitting in the back seat and watching her in the rearview mirror.

She felt ridiculous and weak. "I'm okay," spilled effortlessly from her lips.

"I know you are. I just wanted you to know that we're here too."

Meghan, not known for her shy questioning, looked over at Kim and said frankly, "We're here?' Are you guys a couple or what?"

Kim started to laugh.

"What? Seems like a fair question."

"It is. It is. It's just that we get it all the time."

"So...what's the deal?"

Tony answered for them. "I'm gay."

"Oh. I guess that would be a no then."

Kim smiled and corrected them both, "Tony is the best boyfriend that I've never slept with."

Tony, speaking more effeminately than Meghan thought possible for a man of his frame, gasped, "Oh stop," and then laughed. The two women quickly joined him, their laughter drowning out the monotonous drone of a voice on the radio. The next sputter from the engine caught all their attention and stifled the laughs as quickly as they began.

Tony touched her shoulder again and said in his more usual bass voice, "It's going to be okay. We're gonna make it."

Chuckling uncomfortably, Meghan countered, "Make it where?"

"Wherever we stop is where we're supposed to be. You can trust in that."

Meghan wasn't sure what he meant, but realized that it didn't even matter. She was just glad that her two companions were with her. The third and then the fourth sputters caused her heart to skip, but she felt a little better. She pressed the button on the side of the two-way radio and said to Neil on the other end, "I think we got a problem."

21.

D
r. Caldwell, still wearing his dirt and blood stained lab coat, leaned toward the open side door of the helicopter. Knowing their predicament of fuel, the pilot chose to keep their altitude conservative so that when they did have to land or possibly crash, they wouldn't be that far from the ground.

The day was rising slowly, autumnal laziness winning out over fading summer enthusiasm. Under different circumstances, this would have been a great day; clear, crisp, calm. The doctor thought back to past mornings wearing the same trappings. Memories flashed in his mind like drinking coffee on his family's backyard deck; enjoying the peace before his wife and children arose from bed; absorbing those first moments of day and savoring them for himself. It was different today. Any sense of tranquility or even contentment melted away with a simple glimpse below them. The memories were crowded out of his thoughts by the concern that he harbored for his family. Luckily, his son and daughter were both out of state attending college, but his wife was still at their home on Lower Hillside. He knew that, for the time being at least, he had to focus on the immediate needs of himself and those around him.

By the time they had finally been lifted off of the roof of the hospital tower, the bedlam that had started in an examination room near the Emergency Ward was spreading in both directions on the north and southbound Seward Highway. But like mercury, that sleek quicksilver seeking in every direction at once, the crisis was spreading and deepening and growing. There seemed to be no stopping it. The roar of the turbine engine and spinning rotor blades overhead thankfully muted the carnage.

Parking lots, sidewalks, streets, and stores, everything... there was only death and dying. And the tragedy was that nearly every person dying brought another walking in death. They passed overhead a police roadblock of perhaps six squad cars just as it was being overwhelmed. There was shooting and running and dying, but still the slaughter continued to spread unabated. Further south on Lake Otis, another larger roadblock was taking shape. There were more than a dozen cars and scores of officers, most armed with shotguns, setting themselves into position. He wished he could yell down to them that there was no stopping this. The best they could all hope for was to get out of the way and hope that the storm will pass.

Stan, the co-pilot with the bite on his hand, appeared to be holding his own for the moment. Though wrapped in several layers of bandages, blood still seeped mercilessly from the wound. Dr. Caldwell, regardless of the other man's attitude and dedication, knew that soon Stan would get sick, become sicker and all but incapacitated, die, and then reanimate. There didn't seem to be any reversing the process. For the time being though, Stan was doing what he could to help and Dr. Caldwell decided that he could let the inevitable cook on a back burner.

The pilot pointed out toward the west at an open field just south of O'Malley Road, a four-lane highway of sorts in South Anchorage. The field had what appeared to be soccer goals on it, but it also appeared to be largely flat and open. It was also still far enough away from what was happening that their group stood a fair chance of being able to get away. They were just moments away but the desperate flashing of a red light on the pilot's control panel and a sudden loss in enthusiasm by the motor led the doctor to believe that they might not make it.

The helicopter's turn was sudden and direct. The pilot said "sorry" into his microphone headpiece but only Dr. Caldwell and Stan could hear it. Both helicopter crewmen flicked switches and turned dials as they tried to coax enough fuel and momentum out of the bird to get them to the field.

Dr. Caldwell knew immediately that they were out of fuel and the landing ahead of them would be rough at best. He instructed, with hand signals, the other passengers to strap themselves in and brace themselves for a crash. One woman grabbed an extra helmet from an open stowage compartment and pulled it over her well-sculpted hairdo. She took off her glasses and put them in the front pocket of her silky jacket. Her eyes caught the doctor's and they paused. They didn't say anything, not that either of them could hear it anyway. Dr. Caldwell nodded and forced a smile, which she returned. A sudden jolt from the struggling aircraft erased both of their smiles though as quickly as they appeared.

The helicopter's engines gave out just as they crossed over O'Malley Road. The pilot conducted a controlled but powerless landing, trying to soften the impact as much as possible. Even so, when they hit it was violent and jarring to everyone onboard. The passengers in back were jolted but, for those able to use them, their safety harnesses were mostly effective in keeping them out of harm's way. Equipment fell against them hard eliciting screams and cries, which the doctor could hear again in the absence of any engine noise. Falling on its side as it finally came to rest, the helicopter was immediately smoldering and threatening to begin to burn.

Shaking his head clear, Dr. Caldwell hoisted himself up and peered out the open side door that was now facing up to the sky. The acrid smoke beginning to fill the cabin, climbed out the door allowing the air to clear enough to breathe without coughing. The doctor leaned forward into the stubby cockpit. Stan was quite obviously dead, his neck broken and twisted horribly. The pilot, whose name the doctor still did not know, was unconscious and slumped forward in his seat. Much of the nose of the craft had been crushed inward, concealing the crews' legs. He heard the spark and fizzle of electrical fuses as they one by one burned out.

"Okay, we don't have much time. We all know what we need to do. Let's get out and keep moving." He looked back at the others to register a response. He saw three faces looking back at him: the woman wearing the crew helmet, Officer Ivanoff, and another woman wearing blue nurse's scrubs. A fourth person, another woman, was crying softly and holding her leg. There had been three others in the helicopter when they left the hospital.

He looked around and found a pair of legs protruding from

beneath a pile of heavy equipment that had fallen. He touched an exposed ankle with his first and second fingers and felt no pulse. Where were the others he wondered?

Officer Ivanoff, unlatched his harness and then set about helping the others with theirs. They climbed out one by one while Dr. Caldwell attended first to the woman with the injured leg and then he tried to get an angle to help the pilot. The quarters were agonizingly cramped, making it almost impossible to do anything. The pilot's pulse was strong, but he still evaded consciousness. Attempts by the police officer and the doctor to free the trapped man were to no avail.

"Well, what do you want to do Doc?" asked the police officer as he reached back into the cabin from his straddled perch on the outside of the aircraft.

Dr. Caldwell wasn't sure. He looked all around for anything that might be able to be used to get some leverage. He was still looking when he heard the first sound come from the cockpit. Assuming it was the pilot, he said over his shoulder, "I'll be right there buddy. Hang in there."

He finished rummaging through a compartment, looking for any last remnants of supplies that he could forage.

"Hey, I was hoping that you might be able to help me with the radio. Maybe we could call..."

It was then, in mid-sentence, that he realized that it wasn't the pilot that he was hearing. It was Stan who was still sitting in the co-pilot chair. He was still strapped in and aligned to be facing forward, but his neck was broken and twisted in such a way as to have his head hanging loosely on his right side and looking back at the doctor.

Seeing the doctor with his hungry eyes, he began to gnash his teeth and reach forward trying to grab him. Luckily for the doctor, the direction that Stan's eyes were looking and the direction that his hands were reaching were opposite from one another. The creature was unable to make the connection. He became desperate, shaking his seat and creating a horrible sound that chilled the doctor to his very soul. He was immobilized, a virtual deer in the headlights. And his eyes...there wasn't a shred of humanity in their darkness. Behind the black expanded pupils lurked a preternatural hunger whose shadow was made all the more dark by the translucent hot rage glowing in the white corneas around it.

The absolute fear that gripped the doctor sickened him, weakened his knees, and made his head swoon. He had no will whatsoever. He had felt like this, to his knowledge, only once before and it was when he contracted malaria while he was in Madagascar. The fever damned near cooked his brain. He remembered lying on his cot and hearing the drips of sweat that ran down his arms and legs and fell to the floor. He could hear each individual drop as it splashed in the ant-sized swimming pools his sweat was forming on the floor under him. At night, when the sweating and fever really applied themselves, he could swear that it sounded like it was raining under him. Yet, he couldn't hear anything anyone said to him and barely registered events as they unfolded around him. Often he felt like he was floating and merely a spectator...counting the drops of water as they fell. It was the closest thing to an out of body experience he could claim to have had.

It took Officer Ivanoff reaching back inside to investigate the doctor's delay and that sound to jar Dr. Caldwell from his trance. The police officer shook the doctor and then began to pull him from the craft. As he finally emerged, Dr. Caldwell started to struggle to go back inside.

"The pilot. The pilot is still alive. I've got to get back in there."

It was at about that time that Stan, or more to the point that thing that used to be Stan, was finally able shake himself enough as to readjust his head and neck. With still no bones to hold his head erect, he swung it around so as to be able to get closer at the warm flesh that his heightened olfactory nerves in his nose smelled. Looking like a bowling ball in a pair of nylons, his head dipped and bobbed until he found the right angle to be able to sink his teeth into his former partner's shoulder. He bit through the pilot's jumpsuit, undershirt, and the skin beneath. Thankfully, the pilot never regained consciousness as the geysers of blood from his torn arteries sprayed themselves across the inside of the large helicopter windshield.

From atop the side of the crashed helicopter, Dr. Caldwell could see two other lifeless bodies lying close to one another on the soccer field. He looked more closely, hoping to catch signs of life. When he looked at Officer Ivanoff though, the policeman shook and bowed his head. The doctor knew that could mean only one thing: two more bodies and two fewer survivors.

Falling onto his hands and knees beside the aircraft, the doctor was at a loss as to what to do. In his head swirled a confusing mix of anger, doubt, fear, and a host of other emotions along with the most recent image of horror he just witnessed in the helicopter. What was happening? Where could they go now? Would there be any end to this? He dug his fingers into the still dew damp grass and soft, moist soil. The cool morning air kissed his neck and chilled the beads of sweat still standing there and brought the hair on his arms and back to full attention.

And then he heard it again. For what seemed to be the millionth time yet that day, someone said to him, "Doctor, I think we have another problem here."

He let the defeated, weary laugh creep out of him softly as he remained in the same position. A few tears, those few he still had left in him, escaped to the corners of his eyes and fell harmlessly and silently to the ground in front of him.

He composed himself, putting on his Doctor's Smile and leaned over her. "What's your name?"

Through clenched teeth, the dark complexioned islander answered, "Sulamai. But you can call me Vanessa." She was still rubbing her leg and breathing in quick, controlled, labored breaths.

"Okay Vanessa. Where on your leg does it hurt the most?"

She touched her ample right thigh and said, "Right here. Ooooooooh. It hurt real bad."

The doctor could tell that her leg just wasn't right. Between the angle at which it sat and an alarming knot on the middle of her thigh, he was fairly certain that her femur was broken. He also knew that significant damage to that bone especially could lead to a number of other more serious concerns down the road. Of course, under different circumstances, he'd just order a leg X-ray and help steer her toward a speedy recovery. Unfortunately, these were anything but normal circumstances. In considering their options and needs, he also realized that if they didn't get moving quickly, that damage to her femur would be the least of her concerns.

Dr. Caldwell stood up and, with the ruckus inside the helicopter still serving as his backdrop, he said, "Okay folks, we've made it this far together. We gotta keep pushing." He pointed up toward the park entrance, which was clearly visible and a little less than a mile of gradual incline up and out. "There are houses and people who can help us up that road. We've got to keep moving. Officer, if you and I help Vanessa, I think we can make it. Vanessa, you up for this?"

Vanessa looked up at the doctor and her tears went from those of pain to those of resignation. She shook her head slowly and shrugged her shoulders. "I don't know doctor. I don't know if I can keep going."

Dr. Caldwell, feeling his already diminished reserves of patience fading further, leaned over her and said, "If we leave you here you will die. Do you understand that? And if we wait and debate this any longer, then we're going to die too. I need you to help us so that we can all get out of here alive. Alright?"

She continued to cry and looked back down at the ground. "I weigh more than you and him together. How are you going to move me?"

"We'll figure it out. We've gotten this far haven't we? You ready?"

She took a deep breath and held it but made no move whatsoever.

"Vanessa?"

She thought about her younger sister who was still in school and about her mother who was at home with her younger cousins. She wondered if they were all still safe. Her family lived in the Mountain View area on the northeastern side of Anchorage. Maybe the police would get all of this in hand before it got to her family. She found the small gold crucifix around her neck and went searching for the strength of her Pastor. He always seemed to be so well composed regardless of the situation. Nothing seemed to ever faze him.

"No. Doctor I think I'm just gonna stay right here for a bit. If you get a car and want to come back and check on me, that'd be fine with me but I think I'll stay."

"Vanessa?"

"Doctor we both know full well that I weigh more than both you and Mr. Police Officer Man there put together. There's no point in denying that. You guys'd never be able to move me... not without help anyway. No, I think I'll just stay here for a bit and wait."

"Vanessa, we may not be able to get back down here."

"That's okay doctor. If you can, you know where I'll be."

"Vanessa, I can't..."

She silenced him with her calm expression. If she harbored any fear at all, he couldn't detect it. He was completely disarmed with her resolve. He leaned down and hugged her tightly and kissed her on the cheek.

She giggled playfully and said, "Doctor please. People will talk. I got my reputation to think about."

He smiled at her as he touched her shoulder gently.

She asked, "If you got anything there in that bag to help with the pain, I would appreciate that."

"Sure."

Dr. Caldwell opened the large medical kit from the helicopter and found a syringe with painkiller in it. "D'ya want me to do it?"

Never losing her smile she answered, "Yeah, if you could. How many of those things are in there?"

He handed her two and then one more syringe, suspecting what her intentions were but not wanting to confirm. Hippocrates just did a somersault in his grave.

"Yeah, I'll sleep good with these won't I?"

The doctor nodded his head as he injected the first tube into her leg.

She looked at the four survivors from their small group and said, "Good luck and don't you all worry about me. I'll be just fine."

The four remaining survivors from Providence Hospital trudged up the paved road leading away from the soccer fields and toward the traffic light at the entrance to the park. The pavement was damp as were the waist high plants and bushes to either side of the road. There were scores of geese on the open field and a fenced baseball diamond to their right. Their honking, typically considered obnoxious by the doctor, was a welcome reminder of more normal times. The geese, as if nothing out of the ordinary was happening, were just enjoying a brief stopover in Anchorage as they made their way south for the winter. The doctor wondered what the geese would see when they got to their final destination. Was this happening elsewhere or just in Anchorage?

22.

Neil and his group were just getting themselves out of harm's way when the storm of destruction started to reach them. Luckily, Meghan was able to cajole her car enough to get it off of the Old Seward Highway and onto a side street that opened into a neighborhood of houses and duplexes. It was just another typical Anchorage neighborhood; well, it would have been. Most of the homes looked as if they had been constructed during the Eighties, many showing the wear of the past decades.

It had all the feeling of a ghost town though to all of them. There were open front doors and garage doors all up and down the street, there were clothes strewn across lawns, children's toys laying on their sides in driveways, and, most strikingly, absolutely no people. News of the unfolding disaster must have reached the residents and encouraged them to get away, despite the broadcast's simple message of get inside and stay inside.

Meghan's car came to a rolling stop. She jammed the gearshift into park even before they were completely stopped. Tony and Kim could tell immediately that this was a frustration that wasn't new to Meghan. She turned the key in the ignition and gently tapped the gas pedal the way that Landon, her boyfriend, had done in the past to try and convince the car to start. It hadn't worked any better for him than it was for her right then. The engine sputtered and coughed, but there was no starting it. Not now anyway. If she were able to sit and wait, the car would start readily in about fifteen minutes. Judging by the rising din of noise coming up behind them, she didn't think that she could spare even fifteen seconds. She knew that it was time to give up. She looked over at Neil's minivan, which was even then reversing toward them.

Over the radio, Neil's voice pleaded, "Get yourselves outta there. Leave the goddamned car!"

He was right and Meghan knew it. She grabbed the keys from the ignition, stuffed them in her pocket, and asked, "You two ready?"

Like panicked rodents scurrying from the light, Meghan, Tony, and Kim leapt from the stalled car and ran in search of safety and a place to hide. Neil slowed the reversing minivan and looked over his shoulder at his scared passengers already in the rear of the vehicle.

"Make some room. We got company joining us."

There wasn't really any room to be made though. The minivan was full. Jerry and the two kids pressed themselves as far to one side of the bench seat as they could. In the end, they just moved into the small space between the bench seat and the passenger side sliding door. Jerry was standing but was stooped at the waist. Jules and Danny cowered beneath the arch that Jerry's leaning upper torso created. There was no getting in the backseat as it was filled very nearly to the ceiling with supplies.

Meghan, perhaps involuntarily but most certainly unbeknownst to her while she did it, let out a shrill scream as she ran to the other vehicle and didn't stop until Tony pulled the driver side sliding door shut behind him. Looking around at the others, she laughed and cried at the same time. She nodded to Neil and then let the tears take her all at once. As the tension, anxiety, and fear tickled all of her nerves and senses at the same time, she quaked and shuddered all over at once.

Jules began to cry too. Already pressed against Danny, she laid her head on his chest looking for some comfort...any comfort. She was so confused and now with this lady crying, she just couldn't control it anymore. And not knowing why she was crying made the tears come even easier.

A bitter, heavy and humid sorrow filled the van as they made their way into the neighborhood. It was a fitting soundtrack for their trek and the day that was still unfolding. It was still early enough in the morning that most people would just then be starting their day. Of course, for all of them in the car, the day had already been long and full.

The refuge they sought was there in that neighborhood. The house sat on a cul-de-sac at the terminus of a dead end residential street, which was just around the corner and still in sight of Meghan's abandoned car. There were trees and large hedges in most of the yards. One house, the largest on the street, had a carefully laid pile of enormous stones on either side of its driveway. The house they finally settled on was chosen for the simple reason that its garage door was standing open. Apparently the owners had fled in a hurry, much like the majority of Anchorage residents. The front yard and driveway was littered with hastily packed suitcases with shirt sleeves and pant legs hanging lazily out of partially opened seams. In the backyard barking, was obviously the family dog, confused as to who all these people were and where its humans might be.

Rachel, Jules, and Danny went inside to some upstairs windows that overlooked much of the immediate neighborhood. With the kids still looking out, Rachel went to the kitchen and started foraging through cabinets until she found what she sought. She pulled a big, more than half full one and three quarter liter bottle of Stolichnaya Vodka from a cabinet and took a long and full drink directly from the bottle. The liquor hit her empty stomach like a hammer and sent her to the floor partially gagging almost immediately. She had had enough and the vodka was the final straw that broke the proverbial camel's back. She started to cry and, in trying to fight back the tears, her crying became sobbing.

The others, still in the garage, started unloading the minivan and stacking its contents into semi-organized piles...guns and ammunition to one corner, food and water in another, and miscellaneous materials such as batteries, blankets, flashlights, matches and whatever else in still another pile. Neil looked around at the others and asked, "Who is willing to help me go out back and bring firewood inside?"

Meghan stood back up from the pile of firearms and, dumbfounded, asked, "Are you outta your fucking mind? You're the one that told me what was going on and you wanna go back out into it?"

"It's going to start getting cold at night and we've got no idea how long we will be on our own. I think we oughta get as much wood inside now before..."

"Before what?"

Neil looked at Jerry for confirmation of his fears. Jerry nodded and continued for Neil, "It's just a matter of time before those things realize we're in here. This is a good place...only a couple of windows down low, a fenced back yard, and a fireplace. That's all good. But he's right. We've gotta be ready to be in here for a bit so that all of this can settle down." Jerry knew though that there really wasn't any possibility of "this" just going away. None of the movies or games that he had seen involving zombies had ever ended well. He at least held some small comfort in the fact that he and Neil knew what was happening. In the movies and even in the games, the characters never seemed to have a clue. Maybe that fact alone would be enough to carry them all through this. Neil was right though. They needed to do what they were able while there still was time.

Jerry, Tony, and Neil hurried into the backyard. The woodpile was just outside the door, which was good news. Neil started to toss logs into the garage while Jerry looked around the backyard. He headed toward a small storage shed without doors near the edge of the fenced yard. While his heart was threatening to crawl out his mouth, the six-foot wooden privacy fence lent a small degree of comfort. He looked over his shoulder as he crept forward. Tony stood watch with one of the shotguns at the ready in front of him. Neil too was armed with a handgun slung in one of the shoulder holsters he'd grabbed at Fred Meyer. He was grabbing and throwing pieces of split birch, but looking up every few seconds to scan the fence for any threats.

While they did that, Meghan and Kim went through the house to find any containers into which they could collect water from the faucet. Neil was concerned that they would soon lose electricity and then water service as no one would be left to operate those utilities. Rachel, Danny, and Jules turned on the television and radio to see if any news was forthcoming yet.

In the shed, Jerry found a small stash of lumber, scraps of two by fours, two by sixes, and some pieces of plywood. All of this was carted into the garage as quickly as possible. With some of the firewood and lumber having been moved inside, a fairly hysterical Rachel, who was still drinking from the bottle of vodka, suddenly summoned the three men upstairs.

"Oh my God. Get up here quick! Hurry!"

Jerry all but leapt up the stairs, barely touching foot to carpet. They could see, through a space between trees, the Old Seward Highway where it passed by the little neighborhood. There were still a couple of cars that were trying to make headway, but the vast majority of what they saw were people...hundreds of them, streaming like a chaotic parade down the road. They all heard that train-like sound that actually rumbled and shook the house with the same force as a small trembler. Interlaced in the deep roar, just below that rumbling surface of sound, were barely discernible screams and shouts.

Meghan ran down to the front door and was all set to open it. She yelled, "We gotta do somethin.'"

Both Neil and Jerry shouted down not to open the door. Neil continued, "You're right though. We do gotta do something. This house isn't ready yet. We gotta cover those windows downstairs and reinforce that door. We gotta bunker ourselves in."

Disbelieving, Meghan asked, "We're not gonna do anything for all those people?"

Neil answered her with another question, "What do you propose we do? You saw what was happening on the overpass I'm assuming? There were hundreds of people there and they weren't able to do anything. What can the six of us do? Besides, if we were to save someone from over there on the road, how do we decide which one or ones to save? We haven't got room for everyone here. We haven't got supplies to sustain the few of us for any length of time, how we gonna feed more?"

It wasn't like Neil to speak that bluntly or to be that emphatic. He was typically that guy that nodded during office meetings and merely consented to and with the majority on any issues that arose about which he probably should care; so to say that he was uncomfortable in speaking in such a manner was a gross understatement. The looks that he got from Meghan, Rachel, and the confused children only added to his discomfort.

"I'm sorry. I just..."

Before anyone else could speak or for the mood of the room to change, Rachel attacked the quiet, "You're right. And we all damned well know it. Sorry kids."

Jules asked, "Why do you always say sorry after you swear? Wouldn't it just be easier not to swear?"

Rachel responded, "You're probably right kid. So what about it Neil? What do we gotta do?" And she took another quick swig from the bottle. Her face was as red as a tomato, but her mood had thankfully settled quite a bit.

The group set about deciding how to best use the limited lumber and plywood supply. They had enough pieces of plywood to all but cover the only two downstairs windows. They decided to put the plywood on the outside of windows and then use doors taken from inside doorways to cover the inside of the windows. If they could keep the windows intact, the cooler nights might not be so cool inside. Of course the doors would have to be hung later. Their time outside was running out and they all knew it. They worked with the desperation of dike builders along the banks of a swelling river in the midst of a storm. The job was quick and dirty but it was solid. Inside, they worked in pairs to nail two by fours across doorframes. The garage door was of heavy construction and insulated. It appeared strong and resilient.

Danny, perched in the upstairs window, kept a vigilant watch through binoculars on the passing horde on the highway. He stood there watching quietly, never taking the glasses from his eyes. In the background, he could hear the television, which had begun to broadcast again. It was hard for him to watch the television because all the grownups on it seemed so afraid and they kept talking about places about which he had never heard: Knik, Eagle River, Seward, Fort somewhere and something Air Force Base. None of the news seemed good. It was just easier for him to try and ignore the speaking and watch the road for any bad news coming their way.

23.

It had been only a handful of hours since Martin Houser had been admitted to the Providence Emergency Room. Already though, the city was ready to come apart at the seams. The main roads were filling up with cars that sat bumper to bumper, hopelessly trapped in clogged, pavement arteries.

A precious few jets and large commercial aircraft were still able to depart Anchorage from the international airport. Merrill Field, the state-of-the art small plane airport on the northern side of the city and just east of downtown, was already in ruins. There were wrecked planes, smoldering fuel and equipment trucks, burning control and office buildings, and throngs of staggering, broken souls shuffling across the tarmac. Small Cessnas and Pipers and a number of other single-engine aircraft were still coming in irregular waves and trying to land, the pilots obviously unaware of the bedlam unfolding below.

One plane, a single engine Cessna, sprinted down a runway. Out of control and hampered by the added weight of several extra bodies clinging to the wings and sides of the aircraft, the pilot wheeled his plane through a fence opening just wide enough for his exit. Of course, the narrow opening would not accommodate the wings of his plane, so they smashed into and partially through the high stonewall and light poles to either side of the throughway. Emerging like a magician through a flash of smoke and dazzling electrical sparks, the fuselage of the small plane burst into view. All eyes turned to see this latest spectacle. He emerged onto traffic choked Fifth Avenue, a major thoroughfare through downtown and a natural artery out of town. He steered the plane capably at first, but the teetering imbalance of moving the extra bodies was too much. The plane drove into the side of a new shiny Humvee, which was pushed into another large sport utility vehicle that ended up on its side. The result was that both inbound and outbound lanes were blocked and all the cars waiting to get out of town were suddenly trapped.

At first, there was a chorus of horns from farther back down the line of cars. This was soon followed by desperate, screaming voices as those closest to Merrill Field tried to flee from the wave of death that was spilling out onto the road. Men, women, and children abandoned their vehicles and started running. Most fled without direction, just trying to get away. Many were trampled beneath panicked feet. Others were caught and set upon by their assailants.

Some drivers tried to maneuver their automobiles through the maze to make their escape. This only served to tighten the traffic knot even further. There was no control and no restraint from anyone. The police were being victimized at an alarming rate as those men and women tried to protect the civilian population and found themselves overwhelmed time and time again. More and more gunshots rang out as ordinary citizens tried to stand their ground. Many innocent people were wounded or even killed as most of the shooting became random.

People fleeing on foot made their way to the bridge spanning Ship Creek and connecting Anchorage to Elmendorf Air Force Base. Mothers carrying children wrapped in blankets, fathers tugging older children by hand, and individuals all swarmed across the bridge looking for safety.

A pair of Military Police Humvees met the mob approximately halfway across the bridge. The soldiers, armed with M4 automatic rifles, fired their weapons in the air to absolutely no effect. The crowd didn't hesitate for even a moment. They couldn't. There was only the smallest of divides between them and their attackers. If they paused, they would have been caught. The soldiers, twelve in all, let the civilians pass, as if there was any possibility of doing otherwise.

Shortly on the heels of the first group was a second group of people. At least, from a distance they looked like people but

Lieutenant Van Dorffman wasn't entirely sure about that as he looked down his binoculars at them. They looked somehow different. It wasn't just the torn clothing, bloodstains, or odd walking that they did that caught his attention. It was something more about the expressions on their faces that caught him off guard. Even from this distance and through binoculars, he could make out their faded, vacant, and empty expressions. There was not a single indication that any of them were anything more than upright corpses, except for something that boiled around and in their eyes.

As soon as the refugees had cleared their field of fire, the soldiers opened fire. The staccato crack of their gunshots was, at first, reassuring to the survivors now behind their line. Some even slowed their pace and turned to watch the professionals do their jobs. The first rank of pursuers, riddled with crimson patches, fell to their knees but most were quickly up and moving forward again. Even with automatic weapons, body armor, and military training, the soldiers were overwhelmed as quickly as any other force that sought to stand up to the onslaught. Lieutenant Dorffman tried to radio command that their line had been breached, but as he turned away from the utter carnage that was being reaped upon his men, he too was attacked. From his headset com-link that was still open, he broadcast nightmarish bubbling and gurgling as his tongue was ripped violently from his mouth. Death did not come fast enough for the unfortunate young soldier.

There just seemed to be no stopping the infection from spreading. There were fires burning, most out of control, all across the city by now, the smoke adding a constricting pall that laid itself as comfortably over buildings as it did over bodies lying in the middle of streets and roads.

Anchorage was envisioned and created in the second decade of the Twentieth Century and it took nearly a hundred years for the city to become a thriving metropolis replete with modern business and retailers and nearly three hundred thousand residents. Several hours were all it took for this center of population for the state of Alaska to be brought to its proverbial knees. There was no order as most of the police force had been victimized early on trying to stand their ground. There were already ghouls wearing police uniforms amongst the horde of undead, testament to the ultimate sacrifice many of the officers paid.

Several fire stations were identified as safe sites by the radio and, just as Jerry predicted, those stations became beacons for the ghouls. They flocked to the sites like sharks responding to the faint scent of blood in the water.

The Bear Valley Fire Station was the lone holdout, but it was no longer functioning as it was intended. Dozens of people had sought refuge there as promised by the radio. The station head, having lost contact with every other station as well as all other emergency personnel in the city, knew that something had to be done. They could wait and hope for relief or they could flee. He decided to split the difference and do both. As many civilians as possible were loaded onto their biggest engines to make a run for safety. Those unable or unwilling to leave did their best to seal themselves inside the station in hope that help was on its way.

24.

Dr. Caldwell knew that he was out of shape and unfit to really exert himself anymore. He hadn't been athletically active in years and it showed. It was no great surprise then that he found himself out of breath before he had even cleared the first parking lot that was at the very end of a long and steep road leading out of the sports park. The thing that concerned the doctor even more than his own shabby performance was that no one else was even able to keep up with him.

He stood there, panting and out of breath, waiting for the others. He was glad that he had stopped smoking but wished he had done it long ago instead of just recently. He didn't want to quit really, but he just got sick of hearing them complain and point out all of the obvious health threats. "I mean, really Dad, you're a doctor. You above everyone else should know. And what about second hand smoke? And blah blah blah blah." It worked though. He quit a little more than nine months ago and now the craving for a cigarette was the worst that it had been since having quit. It was no use though. He didn't have any and couldn't get any. He might as well just push on past the craving and deal with it.

His three companions, the only survivors to escape the massacre at Providence Hospital, were making their way as quickly as they were able across the parking lot. One of the women, Emma, was still wearing the extra helicopter crew helmet she put on just before crashing. She was struggling to run primarily due to her choice of footwear. She finally stopped and kicked off her high heel shoes, opting instead to run with hosier covered feet. Once done, her pace increased substantially until she was standing next to the waiting doctor. The other two joined them and they continued on, this time the doctor chose to move with the group rather than on his own. He knew that they needed to stay together if they hoped to get out of this situation alive.

They speed-walked up the inclined road toward the main road. Coming from not far away but out of sight nonetheless, they could hear a sound that resembled a train but was not industrial. The sound was full and constant like an engine but was absent any of the typical trappings of a mechanical source. Luckily, it sounded as if the noise was still some distance away. It was, however, approaching.

Officer Ivanoff opined, "It sounds like a stampede." Dr. Caldwell couldn't have summed it up better. It did sound like a stampede; frightened, horrified animals fleeing for their lives. He continued, "D'ya think it's headin' this way?"

Dr. Caldwell was wondering the same thing but also wondered if it wouldn't be better if they were just able to avoid the stampede altogether; knowing full well that the stampede was more than likely Anchorage citizens dashing for safety. There just didn't seem to be any benefit in moving in large groups right now. Sure, there was safety in numbers, but the numbers had to be manageable. He didn't want to be a virtual lemming being run off the cliff.

The doctor told them that he thought they should just find some temporary but safe shelter and wait this out for a while. Directly across from the park was a small neighborhood with two rows of houses facing one another and a single road separating them. That seemed to be their best option, so they headed down the road.

A small Subaru wagon with significant rust around the wheel wells, sped toward them. The doctor stood out in the middle of the road to flag down the vehicle for help. He stood there until the last moment when he realized that the driver was neither slowing nor swerving to avoid him. He stepped out of the way of the oncoming vehicle at the last moment and watched it speed away from them without even looking back. At the stoplight, the car veered sharply to the right and then was out of sight. Further down the road, another vehicle, a smallish sport utility vehicle, screeched out of its driveway and started toward them as well. This vehicle too was screaming up the road at top speed. As it approached them though, the driver slowed slightly and lowered his passenger side window. He shouted, "The End is upon us! Repent!" and then continued away.

It was from the house that the second vehicle appeared that the group finally decided upon to stop. Entering through a backdoor, the four of them paused to catch their breath. Emma went upstairs and turned on a television, hoping for some news. The amazing thing she discovered was that most of the channels still had regular programming. Re-runs of Days of Our Lives still played out on the Soap Network. Hitler was still bombing Leningrad on the History Channel. Rachel Ray was still cooking up some concoction on The Food Network. It was as if life was still proceeding normally everywhere else.

She decided that was a good thing at least. She reasoned that these channels' sources were outside of Alaska. That probably meant that the problem was localized to Alaska and possibly to Anchorage. That seemed like it was a good thing. Maybe it wasn't as bad as it seemed.

Dr. Caldwell checked the phones...out of service. Officer Ivanoff grabbed some bread, some peanut butter, and, lacking jelly, some honey from the pantry to put together some sandwiches. He also grabbed a nearly full bottle of Bailey's Irish Cream and four Styrofoam cups.

The fourth person in their party, a woman by the name of Dana, went immediately to the bathroom and hadn't been seen since, though occasionally all of them could hear her sobbing. It was okay though. They all felt like that. The doctor was just spent emotionally. As he watched the images from the local news network splay themselves across the screen, he might as well have been watching The Food Network or possibly The Weather Channel. None of it was new. It barely caught his attention...until, the reporter began to talk about the line of defense that seemed to be holding.

"What was that last bit?"

Emma, still wearing the helmet, peeked up at him from beneath the red, white, and blue paint on her headgear and welcomed him back with a smile. "They've set up some kind of barrier at the Knik Bridge crossing."

"Barrier my ass. I bet they've blown the bridge. I wonder how long they can hold there? Who's holding there? Is there any news or advice for holdouts in Anchorage?"

"The last thing I heard the guy say about it was that authorities had lost all contact with Anchorage. It didn't sound too good. Sounded like maybe we might be it."

"What about Fort Richardson and Elmendorf?"

"Those that were able were evacuated. There is still sporadic resistance on Fort Rich, but there is no contact with those groups or individuals."

The doctor, impressed by her report, said, "That was very thorough."

"Thanks. I'm a transcriptionist. It paid to have good instant recall."

"I believe that. You doin' okay?"

"Okay? Are you? I mean, what does that even mean anymore? Is there okay anymore?"

The police officer handed each of them a cup with some Bailey's and a napkin with a half a sandwich on it. He said by way of apologies, "It was the best I could do."

The doctor nodded and thanked him. They ate their meal in silence, except for the unfolding news on the television and an occasional sob from the bathroom. Soon though, there was only silence other than the TV.

The police officer, standing at the window, observed, "The days are already getting shorter. It's still early but it'll be dark in a handful of hours. We stayin' here for the night or trying our hands at movin' on to someplace else?"

Emma suggested that Dana be involved in the discussion. They hadn't really checked on her in at least an hour either, so she walked to the bathroom door and knocked softly. No response. "Dana, you okay in there?" Still no response. "Dana?" Nothing.

The two men were already on their feet. While Emma continued to solicit any word from inside, the doctor and police officer leaned into the door and eventually broke it from the simple and insubstantial frame. There, on the floor of the bathroom, lay Dana. Apparently she couldn't face the moment and instead elected to swallow a bottle of pills taken from the medicine cabinet and then cut her wrists with a razorblade removed from a man's razor. On the floor around her was a mixed pool of deep red and foamy, white vomit.

Doctor Caldwell dropped to his knees beside the woman and checked her heart. "I think I can hear a faint heartbeat. She barely has a pulse but it's there."

Emma laid her hand on the doctor's shoulder and said somberly, "Let her go Doc. We don't know what she lost today. Maybe she knew that this was the best thing for her."

The police officer, eyes agape, offered, "But it's a sin. We can't just sit back and let her eternal soul be damned."

The doctor looked at the other man, considering what he said. Emma however was nonplused by the suggestion and decided to fire back. She said, "You think it could be any worse than this? Besides, maybe she didn't buy into that story."

"It doesn't matter whether she believed in the Truth or not. The Truth is just that: Truth. Her belief or lack of doesn't diminish that. As a Christian, I..."

Emma, chuckling lightly, said, "You can still, after all that has happened today, believe in some benevolent God sitting in the clouds on some big Lazy Boy Recliner watching his creation unfold? That is either unshaken faith or just sheer delusion? Either way, I really don't want to hear any more of that horseshit. We got a deal? I won't belittle your mythology and you don't thank or praise God for every Goddamned thing that happens. Kay?"

Stung, the police officer stood up and walked away. Catching the doctor's questioning look, she said, "Sorry. I guess I'll go apologize to him too. I just have to hear that nonsense from a coworker all the time and it drives me crazy. Everything is "we Christians think that..." and "we Christians believe..." I just can't stand hearing it anymore. Especially if the amount of time I got left here can be possibly measured in hours, I really don't want to hear any proselytizing. Is it too much to ask?"

The doctor answered honestly that he didn't know what to think anymore. He was completely distracted and unable to concentrate on anything at hand. Again, he thought of his family. He was glad that his children were away at college already. They were conceivably safe and away from this horror. His concern for his wife was immense however. Maybe she'd been able to get out before all hell had broken loose. Maybe she was able to connect with some other survivors and find themselves a good hiding spot. He doubted it though. This thing had begun at such an early hour of the morning and spread so quickly. He wondered if it would at least be quick for her. He didn't want her to have to suffer. She didn't deserve that. She was just too good a person and wife to deserve it. He also knew though that the kind of death that struck these victims was anything but quick and was nothing but suffering. To be gnawed and chewed and clawed and eaten was hellish. The anguish was inconceivable. He felt sick to his stomach again. They stooped there over Dana for a quiet few moments. Neither of them was sure when heart and breathing stopped, but the next time the physician checked her pulse it was gone. Not even an echo of life.

Emma disappeared for a moment and then reappeared with a sense of urgency to her step. "I think the cop flew the coop. He's gone."

"He's what?"

"He's gone. He's nowhere down here. I went down there to apologize and the front door was open and he's gone."

"And he's got our only gun."

Emma smiled and said proudly, "That's the other thing we gotta talk about." She raised the shoebox she was holding all along and said, "I found this." In the box was a black revolver and a box of shells. It looked like a .357 Magnum; probably a Smith and Wesson. It looked big and powerful and comforting.

She continued, "It was sitting on the table in the hall near the door leading to the garage. Driver probably set it down going through the door and then forgot about it."

Doctor Caldwell smiled and said, "Good find my friend."

Emma smiled and handed the box to the doctor. Loaded and in his belt, the gun did deliver a certain sense of security. He and Emma moved Dana's body to the backyard and covered her with a blue tarp. Neither of them knew Dana. They didn't even know her last name. They stood quietly after covering her and looked down at the blue plastic package. Without a word, the doctor hoisted Dana up under her shoulders and Emma grabbed her feet, each hoping that they wouldn't upset the tarp covering the expired soul beneath. They carried her to the backyard and laid her out near a small garden that was doing its best to yield a modest crop of carrots, cabbage, and lettuce despite the cool air.

Emma asked, "Should we say something?"

He didn't know. He wasn't a priest. In fact, he wasn't very religious at all and couldn't recall any Bible verses to recite. He was just never that interested in church or religion. It just wasn't in his nature. He wasn't one who mocked the religious though. And then it hit him. He looked up from the tarp-covered body and recited, "Life's but a walking shadow, a poor player. That struts and frets his hour upon the stage. And then is heard no more. It is a tale told by an idiot, full of sound and fury. Signifying nothing."

After a quiet few seconds, Emma said, "Kind of nice Doc but kind of cold too."

"It's the best I could do under such short notice."

"Was that Shakespeare?"

"Yeah, <u>Macbeth</u>. I think."

They stood there quietly for a bit longer, Dana's quick memorial service being extended, for each of them, to all those they had seen fall during the day and all those that were to fall in the coming hours and days. The silence was all but absolute. There were neither birds nor insects lending their voices to the day's choir. The doctor looked up at the woman and was going to ask what the plan was now when they both heard that stampede sound again. The sound all at once filled the void and it was getting louder and louder by the moment.

It had been an hour since the police officer made out on his own. Standing on the woodpile leaning against the seven foot cedar privacy fence, the doctor could see the man running as hard as he could trying to get back. And immediately on his heels was a crowd of a hundred or more of the beasts chasing him.

Doctor Caldwell shouted at Emma to get over the fence and set out across the adjacent woods. He thought he could see other houses on the far side of the small wooded lot. Maybe they could get over there and find some safety. If the ghouls could be stalled long enough getting through the fence, perhaps they could get some distance between themselves and their pursuers.

Emma didn't hesitate. She picked up a five-gallon bucket partially filled with birdseed and covered tightly with a heavy-duty plastic lid. She set the bucket against the fence and, using it for an extra lift, hoisted herself up and over. The doctor tried to get the police officer's attention. He shouted, "Go over the fence! Use the bucket and get over the fence! We'll meet you in the woods! Don't look back! You can make it!"

The doctor got down from the wood and then got himself over the fence. He felt better having the storm behind him. The sound was slightly muted thanks to the houses and fences separating him from it. He saw Emma just ahead of him and increased his pace slightly to catch her. She jumped and screamed slightly as he touched her on the shoulder.

They emerged in another neighborhood with another street and more houses. The sound was still behind them thankfully. They were standing in a dead end cul-de-sac that was perhaps five houses deep with three houses situated on the curving court. It was pretty standard suburban planning. It also looked as deserted as the area from which they had just departed.

Emma, out of breath, panted, "Looks like everyone left in a hurry."

"Yeah, a big hurry. Such a hurry that someone forgot their car."

Emma looked at the doctor and then at the gun tucked into his belt. Like a gunslinger walking into the OK Corral, he pulled the revolver from his belt. He pulled the eager hammer back to have the gun at the ready. He knew that it wasn't the safest way to hold the firearm, but he was comfortable with his decision. He didn't feel like he could afford any delays.

With trepidation flavoring each footstep, the two of them moved forward. They arrived at the car without incident. Emma kept an eye out as the doctor checked in the car. It was a little Subaru Forester, an older model but still in very good shape. It wouldn't be a bad car in which to make a getaway.

Meanwhile, Emma heard a sound emanating from behind the closed garage door. She stepped cautiously to the door and listened. Nothing. She knocked two quick raps on the heavy door and waited. Her response was a rasping, guttural, ravenous groan and fingernails clawing at the other side of the closed door. She retreated from the sound as if she had been touched by something very hot or very cold. She turned and saw a disappointed doctor looking at her.

"Keys?"

"I'm afraid not. What's in the garage?"

"I think it's more of those things. Maybe the folks who were loading this car. Maybe they got attacked and retreated into there with one of them already bitten. That one died and then we know what happened. They were trapped and there they stayed trapped."

The doctor added, "Yeah, but the real tragedy is that the keys to this rig are in the pockets of one of those things in there. Right now this car is just a big paperweight. Unless of course one of us wants to go in there and get the keys."

"No, I think that..."Emma trailed off and then continued more hopefully, "Hey Doc, is there a purse in there?"

"Yeah."

"Look for keys in it. Maybe she left hers in there for us."

Leaning in, Doctor Caldwell yelled triumphantly, "Emma you're a fucking genius. You really are."

Their celebration was cut short however when the slanted front panes of glass from the house's south facing solarium exploded outward. The shards of flying glass were followed by a thrashing and desperate ghoul who was made all the more horrific by the dozens of cuts and deep gashes inflicted upon him in jumping through the window. He hit the still moist grass and tried to continue running but, instead, slipped clumsily and fell rolling onto the paved sidewalk. Seemingly unfazed by the misadventure, the creature leapt to its feet and was starting to run toward the doctor who was still leaning inside the car and in shock. Emma screamed for the doctor to do something, anything. He couldn't swing himself around though. He got his hands on the keys tightly, hooked his arm up and around, and then tossed the keys to Emma before the thing could get its hands on him.

Two quick cracks rose above the beast's own bloodthirsty growl and then the thing fell forward, its own momentum carrying it against the side of the Subaru. There standing in the middle of the street was Officer Ivanoff, his sidearm raised and still at the ready. "We clear? Is he dead?"

The doctor inched a little closer to make sure and then said candidly, "He's dead enough for me. C-mon and get us the hell outta here will ya?"

Emma, furious, shouted, "What d'ya mean, 'Get us outta here'? It's his Goddamned fault we're on the run again. Why don't you drive?"

Doctor Caldwell could sense her disapproval and tried to cool the situation with simple logic, "He has been professionally trained to drive in heated conditions. Am I not correct in assuming that?"

The officer nodded.

"So it merely makes sense that he should drive. Let's let each of us do what we're best at and maybe we can all get out."

Not entirely placated but wanting to get away quickly, Emma threw open the passenger door and slumped into the seat heavily and unhappily. Doctor Caldwell climbed into the backseat and Officer Ivanoff sat in the driver seat. The doctor watched out the back window as the first wave of their pursuers was just emerging from the unfenced yard through which the three of them had come.

Immediately after the gunshots, there was a temporary pause in the riot sound coming from the house they had just vacated on the other side of the trees. And then the sound changed and became even more furious. As if they were provoked by the sound...aroused.

The good thing about the vehicle was that there were actually some supplies already in it. Some bottled water, some bread, some canned foods, and some blankets were piled neatly in the trunk area along with some beautifully decorated personalized family scrapbooks.

Still fuming, Emma finally couldn't hold back anymore, "Why'd you do it? You led them right to us. Why?"

Not taking his eyes from the road, he answered, "Those things were after me. What'd you want me to do? They were coming for you too. You oughta be thankful that I shot that thing before it got the Doc. Where'd you be now if that thing got him and then went after you? You'd be on foot right about now."

Nodding her head and laughing, "How many of those things did you run into while you were running back to us? I bet it was a big fat zero because we weren't even on those things' radar. And you had to lead them right to us. We might have been able to stay

114

there until help came for us but now we'll never know because you led them there. What the fuck were you thinking? Did you have a fleeting thought about the jeopardy that you might be putting us in...the people that you are supposed to be protecting and serving? Or were you only thinking about your own ass? "

From the backseat came, "Emma, give it a rest. He was only scared. We're away now and maybe in better shape than staying there. We're on the move and maybe we can find help."

"Yeah, or maybe we'll just get backed into a corner. Trapped."

"It's probably not that bad. Let's just figure out the best..."

Emma had turned and was facing him and Officer Ivanoff was looking at him in the rearview mirror. He exhaled a sigh and said, "Let's just stick together. We gotta watch out for one another so that we all can get outta this. Right now it all looks bad, but we can make it if we work together."

Emma nodded but shot an accusatory glare at the police officer.

Officer Ivanoff didn't say a word. He looked out of the corner of his eye at the woman sitting next to him. Who was she to question him like that? He'd never let his wife speak to him like that. Of course, he and his wife were separated and hadn't spoken in years, but when they were together, you better Goddamned believe that she wouldn't have been permitted to speak like that to him. He chewed his bottom lip while he imagined the things that he could have said or should have said to save face in front of that doctor. Officer Ivanoff was concerned what the doctor thought of him. He didn't want to seem weak or afraid, like that woman suggested.

25.

And he didn't think he had been afraid now that he thought about it. After he left the house, the doctor, and that woman behind, he got out to the main road, where there were some cars here and there but there weren't any people at all. He felt like the last man on earth. He could only think that he was feeling how Adam must have in Eden. Despite all that had happened today and all he had seen, he felt at peace. Those people back there weren't going to save that woman from her horrible mistake. They refused her any chance at salvation because it was just more convenient for them. That woman, Emma, said it was what Dana wanted and to let her be. He was certain it was just because she didn't want to be hassled with having to help her in her time of need. And that doctor...he obviously wasn't moving to help either. Emma probably bewitched him.

Officer Malachi Ivanoff didn't believe in witches spells or magical hexes, either positive or negative. His belief in the paranormal was limited to his knowledge of the Holy Ghost as part of the Trinity. He did, however, believe that there were women and even some men out there who knew how to manipulate and control others. And in so doing, these manipulators could change the minds of some very smart people just through their wiles. He could see it in the doctor's eyes already and the doctor had no idea. So, he knew that the doctor was going to do exactly what she told him to do. Officer Ivanoff just couldn't bring himself to stay with and protect people like that who had no care for the immortal soul of others. So he ran.

As he made his way east on the road though, these thoughts and justifications rambling through his head, he looked out and saw a line of cars that extended several car lengths in either direction of a railroad crossing. It was then that he could hear the thunder of an approaching train. The road in that direction appeared to be blocked to vehicle traffic. He found it odd that the trains would still be running and then began to wonder how the locomotive would get through the intersection with cars across the tracks as they were. He still couldn't see the train coming, but he could certainly hear it. It sounded as if it were coming from the north. The sense of civic duty still a driving impulse in him led him to start running toward the crossing to see if he might be able to move the cars himself.

He ran hard, trying to close the distance between himself and the cars quickly. His surprise registered immediately on his face and his feet struggled to stop when he realized his error. He saw the throng round the corner of the main road, which was still about a football field's length further on than the railroad tracks. The mass of people, roaring like they were going into battle, spilled across the road and the parking lot to the convenience store on the corner. In front of the bloodthirsty mob, there were three people who were obviously being chased by the others.

The two men and one woman were strained to the point of breaking and still they ran. One of the men took a bottle from the pack of the other. He did something to it that Officer Ivanoff couldn't quite make out and then tossed it over his shoulder without even looking. In flight, the officer could see a smoke and heat coming from the bottle. Then it exploded on the pavement into a ball of fire. It was a Molotov cocktail. Maybe it would be enough to discourage the pursuit.

His stomach sank though as the beasts simply ran through the fire as if it wasn't even there. Several of them smoldered and burned as they continued their pursuit. The Molotov cocktail thrower was falling behind the other two. It wouldn't be long for him.

The two survivors ran harder. They saw him. The survivors, the man and woman, spotted Officer Ivanoff and screamed for him to help them. He couldn't understand their words, but he could register a sense of relief in their voices. They'd made it.

Perhaps they were saved. His hand went to the pistol on his hip. He remembered that he only had four rounds left. What help could he possibly be?

He wasn't even in control anymore. He turned, their pleas still echoing behind him, and started to run. He needed to get back to that house with the doctor and the woman again. He couldn't save the man and woman on the road, but maybe he could save the other two. Maybe if he saved them, he might be able to Save them. That woman might be willing to hear him. Maybe.

He just had to run. He had to get away. He moved his legs as quickly as he could, which wasn't very fast, but the distance already between himself and the crowd helped his confidence. He stayed on the road, using the flat and predictable surface to help him maintain a consistent pace. He just had to stay in front of the locomotive sound that was forever approaching him from behind. Was this how those other people felt? He thought briefly about hunters and their prey. He thought about himself and the times that he had stalked a moose or caribou. Had they felt the same fear that was damned near paralyzing him? It was a fleeting thought that barely registered as at the same time another thought flashed through his mind with the brightness of a neon sign: RUN.

26.

And that was exactly what he did. He ran and ran, making his way back toward the doctor and that woman. He needed to get back to them to warn them. He owed at least that much to them. They needed to know about this flood that was approaching. Besides, there was safety in numbers. And that was why he returned to them. He wasn't afraid and looking out for his own hide as Emma suggested. He was just doing his duty and once again he was being criticized for it. Typical. He let Emma's harsh words roll off his back and tried to remind himself that women can sometimes be irrational in tense situations. His wife was an exceptional example of irrational behavior. He was guessing that Emma was too. For that reason, he tried not to take her criticism personally, knowing that it was just her fear talking. Who could blame her really? It's just a lucky thing that he came back for them when he did.

Their car screeched straight up the road until Officer Ivanoff realized he had run them into another cul-de-sac without an outlet. He swung the vehicle around in the large tear-shaped housing court and quickly found another road leading away. He was able to put some distance between them and their pursuers, but between dead end streets, exits blocked with cars, and more cul-de-sacs, they weren't able to find a good way out of the neighborhood. Shifting their focus from trying to get away to merely trying to find some safety, they eventually elected to pull the car into a partially fenced backyard that was more or less out of sight. They hoped that being out of sight might help them to be out of mind as well.

They waited for several minutes in complete silence. They barely breathed so as not to draw attention to themselves. Their hope was that they could become invisible and simply melt away when the time was right.

Doctor Caldwell handed each of the other two a bottle of water. Emma drank from hers greedily and watched out the window intensely. Before she realized it, silent tears were spilling from the corners of her eyes. She didn't consider herself one of those emotional women that cry with the slightest provocation, so she was surprised by the tears. She wasn't even quite sure why she was crying at all. Not that she hadn't seen and felt things all day long that wouldn't justify a few tears.

Officer Ivanoff, still perturbed with Emma's verbal assault, finally looked over at her and saw the tears. That was more of what he expected from a woman: vulnerability. He felt himself ease up on his feelings toward her. Maybe he was right after all. Maybe her attack on him was merely a product of a very tense situation. Maybe there was hope that she could be a good person. He undid his seatbelt and started to lean over to her as if to embrace her and comfort her.

Emma's reaction was not what he expected at all. She immediately withdrew, all but plastering herself to the window and door of the passenger side. "That's why I don't cry. Because people like you think that you can console me somehow. You look at it as a sign of weakness and think that because you sit there stoically unmoved by events that you're somehow stronger than me and can comfort me. I may need a lot of things, but your pity isn't one of 'em."

"Emma!" again Doctor Caldwell tried to play the role of mediator from the back seat.

She turned to face him and continued, "Try and see it from my point of view, Doc. Here is a guy who ran out on us because we hurt his feelings...sorry, I hurt his feelings. And keep in mind that he isn't just some guy. He's a police officer. So he ran out on us and then brought bad guys back to us. And why? Because he's not willing to live by the power of his own convictions or his own pledges. I think I'm allowed a bit of a gripe with him."

Officer Ivanoff, stung again, asked, "What the hell are you

talking about? Convictions and pledges?"

"You're a fucking cop. What were you...?" The tears were coming uncontrollably now, but these tears were heated with anger and not lukewarm from despair. They filled her eyes and obscured her vision. Her frustration and resentment boiled over and took control. She couldn't even verbalize herself anymore. She did the only thing she could think to do. She got out of the car and went into the unlocked back door of the house behind which they were parked.

Completely surprised, Doctor Caldwell unlocked his door and was set to get out but the door wouldn't open. He pulled and pulled on the handle to no avail. The lock was disengaged but the door wouldn't open. Finally, he realized his mistake and asked, "Hey Malachi, can you open my door from the outside please? I think the Child Lock is on."

Officer Ivanoff, still looking in disbelief at the still open back door to the house, responded slowly. He scanned the yard twice, looking for any predators, and then got out. Doctor Caldwell, flipped the switch on the edge of the rear door, so as not to be inadvertently trapped again and then started inside. He stopped, thinking better of it for a moment, and then asked, "You coming? I could use some backup if we run into anything in there."

Looking at the car for a moment before he answered, the police officer, still trying to hide even from himself the shame that was threatening his thoughts, "Yeah, I'll be right behind you Doc."

The three of them spent a quiet several hours together in the upstairs living room of the house. The only sounds in the entire house were the rhythmic ticking of a wall clock and the frantic voices of impromptu news anchormen and women on the television. As night came, they decided that it would just be more prudent for them to sleep in the car. If any of them would be able to sleep at all that is.

They grabbed a few blankets from a hall closet and made themselves as comfortable as they could in the confines of the small sport utility vehicle. When any of them did sleep, it was in fits and starts. There was no real rest during any of that first night for any of them. They merely counted the hours down until sunrise the next morning. There was still something hopeful about a sunrise. Nothing really changed for them, but the sun coming up the next morning at least implied that some things could still be counted on. It was the wait for that sunrise that was the most agonizing for all of them. The longer autumn night was torturous, harboring teasing shadows and alarming sounds.

III

27.

Settled and comfortable enough to talk for a moment, the survivors in the boarded up house sat together in an upstairs living room. At first, the only sound was a collective sigh of relief. The room was filled with questions, though no one spoke. They looked at one another, not knowing where or how to begin.

Meghan broke the stalemate. She asked quite simply, "What is going on out there?"

Everyone's eyes looked from one to the other and to the other until all eyes were looking at Jerry. He didn't like this one bit. He wasn't accustomed to being the guy with the answers. Besides, he wasn't entirely sure that his answer was the right one. What happened if what he thought he knew was actually wrong? And even if he wasn't wrong, could he believe it either? He was thinking those exact thoughts when he began to speak.

"You all've got to understand that I'm no authority on... well, on anything really. I'm a high school drop out who went back to school to get my GED and some training so that I could get a job. That's all. I don't have a degree in nothin'. I'm just a Nurse's Aide.

"I don't know a lot, but what I do know is movies, video games, books, and music." Neil thought to himself that he could tell already that he liked this kid. That list of interests just secured the deal. Neil was also fairly certain that the "kid" wasn't the dullard that he was painting himself to be though. Jerry may have lacked confidence, but he wasn't intellectually impaired.

Jerry continued, "I think what we may be dealing with out there are zombies."

Kim, leaning against the wall, stood upright and asked, "You mean, those monsters that gotta eat brains and walk around like this?" and she did an imitation that more resembled Boris Karloff as Frankenstein's Monster as she moaned "Brains."

"No, not like that at all. If it's easier to believe, just think of them as people that are infected with a deadly and very infectious disease. Only, the infection in these people kills their sense of restraint, of morality, of family, of right and wrong. These people are completely and utterly incurable.

"Oh yeah, and the disease, it makes them all but impervious to pain. You can shoot 'em. You can stab 'em. You can burn 'em. You can cut 'em in half. You can run 'em down with your car. You can do just about anything you can think of and it won't stop them. They might get knocked down or slowed somewhat, but don't be fooled, there's only one way to bring them down."

Tony asked, "Is this where you tell us that the only way to kill them is to put a bullet in their heads and then burn their bodies under a full moon?"

"The first part of that is right anyway. The only way to put them down permanently is destroy the brain. Severe blunt trauma, like a hammer to the head, would work, but it may take more than one whack and you may not have that kind of time. The best thing is to get them at a distance with one of the guns that Neil grabbed. Good thinking Neil."

Neil was standing in the kitchen now. He was drinking from a bottle of water, but really he was hiding behind the water the way some speakers hide behind a podium. He, like Jerry, wasn't accustomed to being in the spotlight. His bottle empty, he went to the kitchen sink and re-filled it from the tap.

Kim asked, "How does the infection spread?"

Danny, sitting quietly and taking everything in, answered, "The bite, right? It's in the bite. If you get bitten, you get the infection and die and then turn into a zombie. Isn't that right Jerry?"

Jules nodded and added, "I think that's what happened to my brother Martin. Does that mean Martin is in heaven with Grandpa?"

Rachel said, "God I hope so sweetie. What can we do then?"

Jerry was shocked that everyone was accepting his explanation of things. There was no dissension whatsoever, despite the fact that none of them had really seen one of them up close. None of them except Neil and Rachel that was and the moment in the parking lot was over before it even started really; a case of very aggressive hit and run.

Neil chimed in, "For now, we treat this like we would any natural disaster. Think of it like an earthquake. We'll probably lose power and water some time soon. We need to fill everything we can find with water until the water is completely gone from the tap.

"Look around and try to find flashlights, batteries, and candles. That includes from the stacks down in the garage. I think if we work together, we can all get through this."

Rachel asked, "How long do you think this will last?"

Tony, walking away from the others and peering out the opaque curtains hanging in front of the windows, said, "I don't know. How long does it take for the world to end?"

28.

It may have seemed like the world was coming to an end, and maybe it was. For the time being, however, there was still quite a bit to be done. The rest of that first day and into the early evening, they all scoured the house, looking for anything and everything that might be useful.

Danny and Jules found some clothes that fit both of them in a couple of bedrooms. It was about then that Neil realized that he was still wearing his tie and work identification badge. Of course his Arrow brand wrinkle-free white shirt was anything but white by then. It was soiled a dull brownish grey with sweat, soot from the fireplace, and dirt from moving the firewood.

He looked at himself in the mirror and laughed. He took off his badge and set it next to Meghan's keys on a small table in the hallway. He loosened his silk Jerry Garcia necktie and undid his shirt's top button.

Meghan, surprisingly playfully, said, "Now you decide to loosen up a little. Make up your mind. Are you a cool-as-a-cucumber business executive who can handle any situation and still look professional and businesslike? Or are you that guy that only owns four ties, one for each day of the week, and hangs them, still knotted over your closet door so that you wouldn't have to learn how to actually tie them? It's hard to get a read on you mister, changing your appearance as you have."

Neil looked over at her and realized she wasn't wearing her Fred Meyer uniform anymore. She found some blue jeans and a comfortable brown sweater that fit rather nicely.

He started to say something but was momentarily stunned to silence when she turned toward him. He felt an urge to splash into the warm inviting waters of her eyes. They were nothing short of intoxicating. He wanted to ask her if she wore cosmetic lenses to allow her to have such exquisitely colored eyes, but it didn't really matter to him. He was perfectly happy with the illusion for the time being.

And that's not to say that the rest of her face wasn't similarly gorgeous. Her skin was smooth and still enjoyed the lingering but fading bronze of the summer sun. Her hair, no longer pulled back in a tight ponytail, was either a light brown or a faint red with strands of golden blonde intermingled here and there, an obvious attempt to make them appear the natural result of exposure to the sun. Like a luxurious red carpet, her smile was full and inviting. He hadn't seen all or really any of this at the Fred Meyer and probably never would have under more normal circumstances. He was seeing it now though, and it was becoming increasingly more difficult to concentrate on anything else. And to further confound his senses, she was surrounded and accompanied by a ravishingly sweet but un-aggressive aroma that made him think of warm summer days.

She was, Neil realized, a very attractive woman. Neil guessed her to be about two or three years younger than him, which meant that she was ten years younger than him at least. He was horrible at those things. He invariably embarrassed himself when drawn into those guessing contests with new coworkers. Age, weight, sexual orientation, astrological sign, political affiliation, or religion did not reveal themselves accurately to him on the biological or metaphysical barometers in his brain. Maybe he didn't get that part of the brain that permitted such activities. Regardless, she was a very attractive young woman who was smiling at him in the hallway. And she wasn't just smiling. She was smiling at him–at least that was what the faulty barometer was telling him.

Like many guys, when he was confronted with such a woman in tight confines he became tongue-tied and uncoordinated in thought and action. Subconsciously, he was probably surprised that he was still standing. If she got too close to him, he was afraid that the vertigo that he was beginning to feel in that sense of anticipation would have him topple over. Starting on more than one occasion to speak, he second-guessed himself and instead stood there silent, waiting for her to initiate the conversation between the two of them. The funny thing about all of his feelings was that he could not deny that he craved them. Watching Lani bounce into the building every morning for more than a year, he had experienced just an inkling of what he was feeling. He had all but forgotten about the butterflies that could dance and twitter in his belly.

There was noise all around them in the house as everyone settled into their accommodations for the night, but in the back hallway, away from everyone else, there was a quiet and somewhat awkward moment between the two of them. It ended when Neil turned around and went back through the door leading into the garage.

Meghan caught him by the arm and said, "Hey, thanks for everything you did for us today."

Neil shook his head and said, "I don't think I did anything other than just run to save my own ass."

"Maybe. But you let all of us tag along and so far saving your ass has saved all of ours too. So thanks.

"Besides, if you were only interested in saving your own ass then you wouldn't have come back for us when my car stalled. You'd have just driven on down the road and left us to fend for ourselves."

Shaking his head and trying to confess as much to himself as to her, he pleaded, "You've gotta understand, Meghan. I don't have all the answers. Hell, I don't even know all the questions. I'm just a guy who's been in a rut of a job for too long and not sure how and maybe even a little afraid to take the next step. And then this all happened."

Smiling, she said, "You act like any of us are that different from you. I'll let you in on a little secret. How you described yourself is pretty much how it stands for all of us. You don't have to have all the answers. You just gotta be willing to try. That's all."

"God I hope it's enough."

"So do I honey. So do I."

The fact that she called him "honey" was not lost on him.

Hearing himself called that warmed him from the inside out and brought a warm, pink glow to his cheeks.

"Maybe you're right, but I can't do this alone."

"And nobody expects that of you. We gotta look out for one another. Gotta be able to count on one another."

She closed the distance between the two of them and wrapped her arms around him. She laid her head, which came up to just below his chin, against his chest. He was afraid that she could now feel and hear his racing heartbeat and think that he might have some congenital heart defect. His fear immediately gave way to the warm satisfaction that he felt with her pressed against him.

With tears in her eyes she asked very quietly, "Just tell me everything's gonna be alright. That the storm will pass and we'll be okay."

He tilted his head and let his cheek rest on the top of her hair and whispered, "Everything will work out. It always does. If nothing else, you can count on that."

"Promise?"

"Cross my heart."

"And hope to die?"

"Not at the moment."

He didn't see the satisfied look creep onto her face as she nuzzled in closer on his chest. They held one another tight for a handful of heartbeats and when they released one another she said, "You might think about a shower stinky."

"What?" And he sniffed himself curiously, wrinkling his nose uncomfortably.

She walked away laughing and feeling, all things considered, pretty good.

29.

The next morning, Neil awoke slowly, reluctantly. He looked around through his sleep filled eyes trying to remember where he was. When the memories of yesterday flooded back to him, he leapt up from the recliner in which he had been sleeping upright. He spun around looking, trying to see anything that he recognized. The darkness seemed so consuming, swallowing him up like the nightmare that had plagued his brief sleep. Then he realized that the nightmare he'd been having was just his memory replaying itself from the previous day's hellish events. His nightmare was actually his bitter reality.

From the couch along the wall came a deep breath as someone in the dark turned over in sleep. He peered through the dark like a sailor into the fog hovering over a reef filled cove. In the very scant light, his eyes adjusted to reveal the outline of a person sleeping. Neil breathed in and immediately new that it was Meghan.

They spent the better part of the night and much of the early morning talking and looking occasionally out the front window. He told her about his divorce and she about her lingering engagement and less than committed fiancé. Other than the fact that the world they had known was unalterably changed and possibly balancing precariously on its last foot, it wasn't a bad night. Though their talk had become quite intimate, they both held any physical intimacy at arm's length. Neil's reservations and Meghan's lingering commitment to a fiancé that was more than likely dead or worse helped to funnel those urges to the backs of their minds.

He could finally make out the outlines of Meghan's face in the very scant light. He stifled an urge to cross the room and kiss her on the cheek. Just seeing her appeared to be enough. Maybe it wasn't all bad after all.

He stretched and yawned. He had to pull the sweatshirt sporting Seminole college in red letters down over his belly. The sweatshirt and jeans he was wearing were found in a back bedroom. Though the clothes were a touch big on his frame, he was thankful the previous night to peel away the grimy clothes that he'd been wearing through the beginning of the tumult.

He wandered out to the dining room and joined Tony and Jerry at the glass top rectangular dining table. Jerry poured a cup of coffee from a white carafe sitting in the middle of the table on a cork pad and pushed the porcelain Mall of America mug toward him.

The younger man no longer in his hospital scrubs said, "Enjoy it. It'll be the last pot cooked with the help of Mr. Coffee."

Sipping the strong, hot brew, Neil asked with his eyes what he meant. To which Jerry said, "Power just cut out and I don't think Chugach Electric is going to be dealing with the outage any time soon."

Standing and heading over to the window, Neil asked, "Are we still alone out front or have They found us yet?"

Tony, who obviously hadn't been awake much longer than Neil and a bit surprised by the casual nature of the conversation, asked the both of them, "What do you mean yet?"

Jerry answered them both. "It's just a matter of time. Before the streetlights went out, I'd been watching a group of maybe five of Them down the road a bit. They seemed to be just standing there...waiting."

Tony asked, his eyes widening, "Waiting for what?"

"I don't know for sure. What I do know is that they're slowly making their way toward us. When the lights went dead, they were milling around about a block away. It's really just a matter of time."

Neil asked, "Where are they now?"

"In the middle of the road. I think they can smell us but can't quite place which house we're in. It's been a very gradual process. I felt like I was back in junior high biology class watching one of those time enhanced videos of a bird hatching from an egg or a plant emerging from a seed. I didn't see them move. I only saw that they were closer."

Tony was appalled, "They can <u>smell</u> us?"

"Yeah. I think it has to be our smell. Maybe it's the noise we make. It could be something else entirely different or a combination of all of those things."

Neil finished Jerry's thought, "But if we think of them as predatory animals, then at least we've got a starting place with how to beat them."

Leaning away from the table as if he was trying to avoid the coming answer to his question, Tony asked, "You plannin' on takin' those things on? I saw what they were doin' to those folks on the highway. I ain't never heard screams like that before."

"It's exactly because of those screams that I want to know how to outwit those things. That's all we got on them. We can't fight 'em...there are just too many of them. We gotta beat them on other terms...terms of our making and not theirs."

Jerry sipped his coffee and began, "While they stood there, they weren't necessarily standing still. They swayed back and forth, like they were on a loaded spring waiting to be released. While they shuffled in their little circle, their legs moved like yours or mine, with maybe a little more stiffness to them. Maybe they're being affected by rigor mortis. Their arms and heads seemed to twitch every now and again and they didn't seem to be able to control it. Even with those spastic tics, their eyes didn't miss anything. They looked into every shadow. I think they're stalking us."

Tony said coyly, "Don't they know there're laws against that sort of thing? I mean what's a guy gotta do to get some peace?"

"I'd tell you to call a cop but..."

30.

During the night, Emma crawled into the backseat to sleep. She didn't really want to sleep any closer to Officer Ivanoff than absolutely necessary. She cried even through her sleep for most of the night. She had never felt such overwhelming sadness and helplessness in her life. The feelings chased her into her dreams and plagued her with the sense of falling and running impossibly slow from a lurking menace. Like a faded memory coming back slowly, the day's light slowly introduced itself. She opened her eyes slowly in the growing light.

It was very chilly so she pulled the throw blanket tighter around her. The two men were still sleeping. Their breathing was heavy and loud in the confines of the car. Despite the breathing, sleeping men near her, she felt completely alone. She started to cry again; a warm, silent cry that hurt her chest. She stifled the sobs fairly well so as not to disturb the two men.

She heard a nearby wind chime begin to sing its stilted tune. She remembered the wind chimes on her neighbor's porch. The old lady seemed to have a dozen or more sets hanging all around; wooden chimes, metal chimes, some glass, some cut in the shapes of fish. The sound could sometimes interrupt an afternoon nap in the front room, but it was never an unwanted interruption. The sound itself was as soothing as a dream.

There was something wrong though. These chimes just seemed too random. Then she looked at the windsock perched atop the storage shed in the adjoining yard. It was hanging loosely, waiting for a wind to breathe into it life. There was no wind.

She started to shake involuntarily. Slowly, timidly, she turned her head to look out the rear window. Her heart sunk. One of those things was in the yard behind them. It was on the small wooden deck and doing very small circles as if it was looking for something. It barely registered that the thing had once been a woman still wearing a bathrobe tied at the waist. It appeared that her right hand was gone and its place was a mess of ruined and raw flesh. At the moment, it wasn't looking in their direction.

Emma said only, "Oh no."

Doctor Caldwell, his eyes just barely cracked open, asked, "What's wrong?" But then he sat up, realizing what exactly could be wrong. He followed her eyes and saw it moving around in the still very limited light of the still waking morning.

He leaned forward and nudged the policeman sitting in front of him. Nothing. He shook him harder. The only response he got was flatulation and a grunt that originated from somewhere deep in sleep.

The doctor was trying not to make any noise and draw that thing's attention. He leaned forward even farther and whispered, "Officer. Officer," and continued to shake him as well.

Officer Ivanoff woke with a start and in a very irritated, loud voice demanded, "What in the hell do you want?"

The police officer immediately remembered where he was and lowered quietly into his seat but it was too late. The former woman loitering in the yard next to them emitted something that might have been the offspring from the copulation between an excited war cry and a voracious nighttime howl. It was a sound that cut each of them to the marrow. It was running at full tilt across the yard in an instant.

Officer Ivanoff turned the key and, to all of their relief, the car started without so much as a cough from the engine.

Emma said, "I love this car."

Doctor Caldwell said as he loaded the big revolver, "I'll get you one when we get outta here. Deal?"

"Deal."

The police officer shifted the car into gear and made a wide turn in the still dew wet yard, losing control just slightly but regaining with ample dexterity and confidence. Emma had to admit that he was a good driver. Still, she held tight to the back

140

of the seat in front of her. Her heart was racing and her breathing was doing everything it could to keep pace.

She held tightly to the handle on the ceiling just above the window. The car seemed to be over corrected and then she realized that it wasn't merely an over correction. The cop was using the car's steering wheel like a gun sight, lining up the front of the car with the woman. Not to be outdone, she shifted her direction just slightly to put her on a collision course with the vehicle. Malachi Ivanoff pressed the accelerator to the floor and the Subaru's engine grumbled deeply.

Emma was screaming for them to stop or veer away; anything really to avoid the impact. She swore that she could see the police officer grinning from ear to ear as the thing's legs crumpled against the car's grill. The ghoul toppled up onto the hood of the car, and, shattering the front windshield, sailed up and over the roof.

With its robe flapping wildly like an expanse of un-tethered terrycloth sails, the former woman spun and thudded across the moist lawn. By the time she came to a halt, the car had turned back out onto the pavement and sped away. None of them in the car could see the beast come to rest twisted and broken. And yet, even with a shattered pelvis and broken spine, she was so desperate to continue her pursuit that she clawed at the soft soil and grass with her still one functioning hand and tried to pull herself along after them.

The car screeched onto the street and fishtailed slightly on the dew damp pavement. Malachi's smile immediately faded when he beheld the crowd of ghouls that was coming at them from down the street. There were hundreds of those angry, hungry, tortured faces approaching them from a mere handful of blocks. He never, for even an instant, slowed the car.

Emma screamed from the backseat, "Are you fucking crazy!?! You're gointa' kill us all!!!"

Malachi ignored the voice coming from behind him. He looked to both sides, looking for an option. They passed a Court and then a Circle with no road leading out presenting itself. Emma was still shrieking like a wild woman when he jarred the car hard to the right. A sign warned him that there was No Outlet, but he saw what he needed.

Dr. Caldwell, never really losing his cool, asked, "Uh, Mal? This seems to be a dead end but we're not slowing. Mal?"

To Malachi, the doctor sounded suspiciously like that computer on that movie about outer space. He thought its name was 2001, but he could be wrong. There was a space between houses where there wasn't a fence. He was hoping to cut across yards and get to the road on the other side. He knew that it was risky, but he was fairly confident that most of the yards in the area into which they were heading were not yet fenced as it was all new construction.

Malachi felt the vehicle easily climb over the substantial curb. They jostled about for a brief moment afterward. Emma pulled her seatbelt on, as did the doctor. She closed her eyes and held her breath.

Despite the calm facade, the doctor was finding it difficult to keep his posterior in position on the car seat. He was pressing with all his might the imaginary brake pedal that was at his feet but to no avail. They weren't stopping. They weren't even slowing.

Maybe Malachi didn't see it. Maybe he thought that he could jump his car, Hollywood action star style, across it. The doctor wasn't entirely sure of the police officer's thoughts. Regardless, the silver Subaru Forester plunged from the grassy yard into the murky water of the drainage ditch that ran along the border's of this line of houses. The spunky little sport utility vehicle tried to climb its way out of the ditch, but found itself marooned between the steep incline of the opposite bank and the soft mud of the bottom of the trench. Its wheels continued to turn enthusiastically in the muck even after it was glaringly apparent that it was going nowhere.

The doctor was the first to react. He unlatched his seatbelt and looked over his shoulder. They had just seconds.

"C-mon guys. Let's get going. We haven't any time. Grab what you can and let's get going."

Neither of his fellow travelers made a move for a second longer.

"Listen goddamnit! I'm not going to get my ass chewed because you guys couldn't get yours movin'! Now get going. They're almost on top of us!"

With that, both the police officer and the medical transcriptionist were jolted back to reality again. Malachi hefted himself up and forced the shattered windshield out of its frame and onto the hood of the car. Emma followed and the doctor got out last, brandishing the heavy revolver they had found. He turned toward the crowd just a scant few yards away from them. He raised the pistol, pointed it toward their pursuers, but then thought better about wasting a precious bullet on something that would neither slow nor discourage the chase.

The trio of hospital survivors ran hard and fast not looking back for even an instant. The ditch proved a surprisingly effective obstacle to the ghouls, who had to end their pursuit and instead milled about around the wrecked car. Thankfully, this circumstance provided the three people a brief reprieve as they made their escape.

Malachi, though, knew that they were in trouble. They were on foot again and he need only remember the three people being pursued by that horde the day before. There too it had been one woman and two men. He wondered if the woman in that group had been as annoying and obviously weak as Emma was. Her nagging and incessant screaming was starting to drive him over the edge. Maybe she was related to his wife. They certainly acted an awful lot alike at times. Emma didn't seem to be Native, but perhaps the relation was distant and Emma only got the most annoying bits of that family's personality.

Breathless and exhausted, Dr. Caldwell knew that they had to find somewhere safe and relatively secure to stop and rest. There were houses all around them, but he had his doubts as to how secure any house would be. Of course, if they were all too tired to continue to run and they were caught out in the open by those things, then a house wouldn't be that bad of an option. How long could they keep running? How long until help would arrive? How long could they stay alive?

31.

"Why don't we just shoot them? It's not like we don't have the guns and the ammo to do it. There are only six of them out there anyway. We could drop those few and maybe send a message to the rest of them."

Tony was getting more and more agitated as he spoke. It was late afternoon and the group hiding in the house had been inside all day. The two kids, Jules and Danny, had entertained themselves with board games in a back bedroom while the adults took turns peering out the windows at the group that was forming in the street.

Meghan answered Tony, "No, now there are seven of them."

"Seven? Where did the other one come from?" he asked incredulously. He had been watching out the window not long ago and there had only been six of the fiends. They seemed to be multiplying.

Kim, sitting on the floor and drinking a beer, said soothingly, "Oh c-mon honey. Have a seat with mama. I'll make it all better." She patted her lap with both her hands and leaned back. Almost as if on cue, the big man hunched his shoulders forward, laid down on the floor, and put his head in his friend's lap. She commenced to stroking his very short hair and humming a tune that they all recognized.

Jerry, who had become the appointed specialist, added where Meghan left off, "No, I think that if we start shooting, more of them will come and they'll keep coming. Our best bet is to let them pass us by...if they will, and then figure out what to do next. We've got a few days worth of supplies here. Maybe if we wait it out, someone will come looking for us."

Rachel chimed in, "I thought there was a bunch of someones already lookin' for us," and she gestured toward the outside.

Jerry nodded and conceded, "Someone who can help us and doesn't want to eat us, I mean."

Kim, ending her humming, asked, "How did all of this start anyway?"

Neil shook his head and walked to the window. He didn't know. The kids and Jerry were at the hospital where all of it started. Danny and Jules kept talking about Martin, Jules' brother, getting bit on the hand and getting sick, but that was no real help. In the end, Neil suspected that it didn't really matter where or how it began. The cold, hard truth was that they were smack in the middle of a horror movie as it played itself out in reality. Other than that, the only other truths worth considering were those that would keep them all alive.

"I think we should start thinking about an escape plan," Neil said to the group.

Meghan looked up at him from her spot on the couch, "Escape? But you said yourself that we should wait for..."

"No, I mean escape in case something happens and those things find us and maybe even get in here."

Jerry asked, "What'd you have in mind?"

Ever so quietly, so as not to draw attention to themselves, they loaded some bare necessities into the back of the minivan. Between the two front seats, Neil placed a shotgun, two handguns, and a pile of boxes of shells for each. He also put the key in the ignition, just in case they were in a hurry.

The rest of the day was spent trying to occupy themselves as best as they could. But really, what does one do when facing the end of the world? With limited resources and virtually no way to get anywhere, what do you do?

Tony sat at the dining room table and wrote a series of letters to important people in his life. He penned one to his best friend, Angie, to whom he first came out. He wrote another to Phil, a past lover who was never really absent from his thoughts. And of course he wrote a letter to his mother. He took his time, choosing what could possibly be the last words by which he would be remembered carefully, sometimes agonizing over a sentence or a phrase until he wadded up the paper and started anew. With so few words and such a lack of space, he wanted each and every syllable to echo with his voice. These would be his testament and he treated them as such. He spent the better part of the day writing those three letters and when he was done, he laid his head down on the glass table and went to sleep.

Rachel sat quietly on a chair in the corner of the living room and continued to drink the bottle of vodka she found in the cabinet. After more carefully examining the bottle, she realized that it was actually a bottle of Spudka, distilled potato vodka. It tasted more like lighter fluid to her than potable alcohol, but it did result in a very welcome numbing buzz as she drank it. She decided that the buzz was more important than having mutinous taste buds threatening to revolt. She was still experiencing a little shock from all that had happened, but she found herself curiously resenting the zombies for deciding to end the world on the same day that she was to get her annual review and the promise of a raise. She was due damnit! She had worked so hard this year and she was due. Everybody in that goddamned office was making more than her and she was poised to do something about it.

She took another sip from the bottle and quickly swallowed the potent liquid. Even with her buzz, the taste was still, to her, obnoxious. It was the kind of taste that caused her jaw to tighten. It had been some time since she had spoken or even stood and she was in no hurry to determine how badly both of those could be given her rising inebriation. So far, she hadn't felt the need to relieve herself, so she was perfectly comfortable with not testing her abilities in either category. Absently, she checked her phone, still attached to her hip, for messages and tried to dial out again. It might as well be a paperweight for all the good that it was doing her. She thought about throwing it across the room in frustration, but Kim standing in front of her suddenly caused her to keep her anger in check.

Kim held out an empty glass and waited. Rachel smiled and poured a generous portion of the fiery, clear liquid, held up the bottle in a friendly toasting fashion, and then took another drink. Kim smiled at the drunken woman with the messy blonde tangled curls, raised the small glass tumbler, and drank a sip herself. For a moment, Kim was concerned that Rachel had inadvertently grabbed a bottle of paint thinner or gasoline to drink. She'd never had straight vodka before and now she knew why. Its transparency suggested to the casual observer that it might actually be smooth and as innocuous as water. The truth could hardly be further from that.

Still, she held onto the glass and walked herself to the bathroom in the master bedroom. There was a large tub with plenty of towels back there and she planned on pampering herself one last time. Luckily for her, the water and gas utilities had not yet stopped working, though it would just be a short while before the battery-powered backup generators would fail at those locations as well. While she filled the tub with hot water, she went in search of a good book. The reality of the situation was that she would have been satisfied with even a bad book, but none was forthcoming. Instead, she found a stack of magazines with titles like <u>People</u>, <u>Us</u>, and, <u>Soap Opera Digest</u>. These would simply have to do for the time being. She piled her clothes in a neat pile next to the tub and climbed into the hot water, which came up to her neck. The heat from the water mixed with the heat from the alcohol in her belly helped to welcome a very real sense of contentment that all but chased away the day's worries and fears. With her head resting comfortably against an inflatable, bath pillow, she tried to embrace the deep breathing exercises she learned some time ago in a martial arts class she had taken with her friend, Desi.

Across the hall from the master bedroom and Kim's moment of peace, there was anything but peace being waged as Jules, Danny, and Jerry were engaged in a very taut game of Risk. Jerry was holding Australasia pretty firmly and slowly expanding by way of southern Asia into Africa. In the meantime, Jules and Danny were fighting it out over Europe and North America and not paying much attention to Jerry's quiet aggression. There were plastic armies stacked all across the globe poised to attack and defend.

Jerry threw the dice and launched another successful and devastating attack against the scant red armies of Danny's imperial forces holding a patch of land in southern Asia. Jerry moved the lion share of his armies into the now vacant land and continued his turn elsewhere.

Jules was merely playing because Danny was. She didn't have any interest in this game, but it was the only one that she recognized of the several on the top shelf in the closet. It seemed a good idea just to be doing something. She watched as Jerry continued to play out his bid for world domination. She looked away from the game board, not at all concerned that she might miss one of Jerry's moves that impacted her own tenuous hold on southern Europe.

Deciding that not having a barking dog in the backyard to draw attention to their sanctuary was in their best interest, the dog was brought inside to be with all the visitors in his house. Now, he was curled contentedly next to Jules who was even then stroking his ears and neck. He was a mutt for sure, but had the size, fur, and friendly if a little hyperactive disposition of a border collie. His confusion had given way to contentment as he enjoyed the attention of this new little girl.

While all of this was unfolding, Neil and Meghan, having found a stash of miniature Hershey chocolates hidden behind a stack of plastic bowls and tubs with lids, sat themselves on the stairs and indulged their sweet-tooths. They didn't say much to one another but took turns feeding chocolate candies into each other's mouths. Neil wondered to himself if they would ever get out of this situation alive. He munched on a Krackle bar, enjoying the crunch of chocolate covered rice crispies, and looked around. The house around them was as much a prison as it was a sanctuary. It wouldn't take long, he realized, for the walls around them to begin to threaten the fleeting peace they had found. And then what? Would they put to the test Sartre's supposition that "Hell is other people" or would they, given the gravity of their situation, be able to see through any petty differences and come together to survive? Of course, only time would tell. He would just have to wait and see, just like the rest of them.

32.

"We can see them now sir. They're heading our way," the voice on the radiophone reported the update without any sense of fear or doubt. He might as well have been reading the nutrition label from a box of breakfast cereal.

"Okay son. We'll get some gunships airborne and headed your way asap."

"Thank you sir. We'll hold them here for as long as you need."

All eyes in the command center were fixated on the Colonel as he set the radio receiver down. They all realized that it could very well be any or all of them on the other end of the radio. Could each of them be as cool as the disembodied voice circling the communications room?

The colonel stood facing the wall for a moment or two longer without turning to face everyone around him. He was having a difficult time focusing on the task at hand. It wasn't a simple matter of a military operation. He was faced with a confusing and seemingly spontaneous uprising with very few options to end it. Both military bases on the north side of Anchorage were in ruins and going through final death throes. Most of the heavy equipment that should have been at his disposal was either still serving with troops in the Middle East or was sitting uselessly in garages and motorcades on Fort Richardson. More pressing on his mind though was the fact that his wife was on the wrong side of the military cordon that was currently straddling the

Glenn Highway as the only force standing between the chaos that Anchorage had become and the rest of the state. He could order a helicopter and a rescue team to their house to retrieve her, but if he couldn't do that for all of his officers and soldiers in his command, then he couldn't do it for himself either. His wife, a stalwart of fairness and consistency, would be the first to point that out to him. He could picture her saying it as he stood there. He could also hear her reminding him that the quicker he got the job done, the quicker he could move on to worrying about something else. He was an enduring worrier and life just had a way of producing things about which he should and could worry.

He finally looked over at another officer and asked, "How much longer until the bridge is ready?"

As a last resort, the colonel had ordered the destruction of the bridge spanning the Knik Arm waterway, a narrow but effective natural waterway that separated Anchorage from the fertile Matanuska Valley and its roads that connected with the northern two thirds of the state. If the disturbance was to cross the Knik on the existing bridge, it could spread in any direction and the colonel would be powerless to stop it. As it was, the Glenn Highway was cut between the Chugach Mountains and served as a funnel to the Knik Arm crossing.

He hoped that he could disperse the crowds when they saw the soldiers at the blockade and then set to sorting out the madness that started all of it. So far, responses to the tumult had been piecemeal and very ineffective. Deployed across the Glenn was an ad hoc battle group of more than one hundred soldiers and the few Stryker armored vehicles available to him, a very intimidating if a little bit of a ragtag body of men and machines. Having the helicopter gunships hovering overhead should help to convince the leaders of the uprising to withdraw and start seeking different options to settle their grievances, whatever those might be.

He heard the whirling chops of the helicopters as they flew out toward the roadblock. Almost immediately afterward, he could hear the distant pop and crack of small arms coming from his men on the line. The firing rose to a crescendo almost immediately and maintained itself at a furious pace.

He took a deep breath and said, "I need to get up there and see things for myself. Get me a chopper."

33.

On the ground at the roadblock, the major in command peered through his binoculars at the approaching horde. But they weren't just approaching; they were running hard and fast right at them. Many of them, he could see, were wounded or at least had blood on them. More importantly, he could see that this wasn't a small group of ethnic dissidents trying to dismantle the United States or at least Alaska by disrupting communications, shutting down utilities, and spreading fear amongst the population. The group, at least in his eyes, was a perfect cross section of ethnic groups that represented the population of Anchorage and Alaska as a whole. Everyone appeared to be represented.

Ringing in his ear were the rumors about what had happened. Mass murders. Mutilations. Cannibalism. He'd always said that in every rumor there was a kernel of truth. But what of these rumors was true? Was any one more appealing than the others? What horrible truth was propelling these people?

There were still some abandoned vehicles here and there along the road. He was amazed to see the cars disappear under the surge of humanity as if some huge valve had just been opened and the screaming masses poured forth to swallow everything in its path. At first simply piling onto and over the cars and trucks, soon the tsunami of people was carrying the automobiles along with it like a stick riding the current in a storm drain during a spring rainfall. The wave reached as far back as he could see. There were thousands of people coming right at him and his men;

more than he could believe and certainly more than he had been told to expect. He thought to himself, *Christ oh Mighty*.

"Steady men. Hold your fire until the order is given. Maybe we can turn these folks away without having to get heavy with them."

His soldiers, posting themselves behind the hastily prepared defenses of concrete traffic barricades positioned side by side across the highway, readied their firearms for action and waited. He looked at them and could feel his heart begin to wane. Even if he and his men could hold these people at bay, he wasn't convinced they had enough bullets to be able to shoot all of them.

He looked over his shoulder at the open road behind him. He could just climb in the Humvee on which he was standing and drive away. He could stay in front of this mob and never look back. He was sweating now. He could feel it running down his back between his shoulder blades and taste it on his upper lip. He had all but convinced himself to do it...to just drive away as fast as he could, when he heard it.

Preceding the masses was the sound of a freight train. The noise, corralled as it was by the mountains, grew in intensity with each passing collective breath of the awaiting soldiers until they could all feel it. Trying to be heard above the din, the major used a bullhorn to talk.

To the mob he calmly said, adhering to his training, "Please disperse."

And then, "Ladies and gentlemen, this is the United States Army. We require that you disperse and return to your homes at once."

Taking a deep breath, the major almost pleaded, "Please turn around and return to Anchorage or I will order my men to fire."

Seeing the soldiers and hearing the voice, the crowd only became more agitated and grew louder, their hungry groans becoming ravenous growls. They were a scant few hundred yards away when the major ordered his men to fire a warning volley above the multitude's heads. Several other soldiers fired tear gas into the bedraggled ranks as well. None of which had the slightest impact on the throng's progress. As if it knew its potential to turn a bad dream into a nightmare just by its presence, the smoke from the gas canisters clung to the ground and reluctantly rose up in dissipating swirling wisps, fading like second guesses.

The major licked his lips and got a full dose of salty fear. He then ordered, "Okay boys! Let 'em have it!"

There wasn't a moment's hesitation. Every gun in the firing line began to chatter and spit. It was like the sound of a chainsaw cutting into a log instead it was actually the lines of people coming at them. To the major's amazement, the first mixed and disorderly rank was hurled back, but the majority of those hit were back on their feet almost at once to rejoin the others as they continued forward despite the storm of lead lashing into them. Through his binoculars, the major could see with magnified clarity that the bullets his men were shooting were finding their marks. There was a steady red misty wet cloud that hung about the perpetually changing front rank as bullets punched holes in chests, arms, and legs.

There was something very wrong. His men were expending huge amounts of ammunition and a mere handful of bodies were lying lifeless on the road. Despite their best efforts, they couldn't stop the rush. At about that moment, thankfully, a pair of Blackhawk gunships roared over their heads. A third helicopter was still approaching from a little farther back. The relief he felt cannot be expressed in words. Perhaps they would be able to get through this.

He shouted, trying to encourage his men, "Pour it on. Drive them back. Hold your line. Maintain your fire." The major moved up and down the line ordering, hoping, helping. He watched the helicopters rain down fire and destruction.

Yellow, orange, and black flowers of fire erupted up and down the highway. Bodies were tossed through the air with each successive explosion. Unfortunately, most of those bodies again lifted themselves onto their feet and continued forward. More than a few victims were engulfed in flames and then they too arose and carried on, smoky contrails in their wake.

This time the major said it, "Christ oh Mighty."

His radio began to squawk wildly but he couldn't understand it. He tried but he just couldn't focus on anything but what was unfolding in front of him. There was little more than a football field of space separating him from the monsters still coming at him.

Again the radio made a sound. This time he concentrated on the voice coming out. It was the colonel. He said with a crackle of a voice, "Sir, I don't think we can hold."

"I'm above you right now major. Your boys are doing a fine job. Keep it up major."

"We don't have enough ammunition to keep this up sir."

"The engineers just need a few more minutes to prepare the bridge for demolition. Do you understand major? We need you to hold for as long as you can. If they get through and that bridge is still intact, I'm not sure where or if we could stop them."

Banishing the thoughts of escaping from his mind, the major said somberly, "I understand sir. We'll hold."

"Thank you son. If we can keep the fire up from here, maybe you and your boys could save some of your ammunition."

"I don't think that is going to work sir. But we'll do our jobs. Make sure that bridge gets blown."

He climbed up into the gunner's position of the parked Humvee and pulled the hammer back on the heavy machine-gun on the mount. He begged quietly, "Lord have mercy on my soul."

His machine-gun, loud as it was, was barely audible over the already deafening cacophony. A few of his bullets struck his targets in the head and those targets actually fell and didn't get back up.

He paused and decided to aim the gun a little higher and intentionally hit his victims' heads. Again, this seemed to work, permanently knocking down these attackers. He said to himself, "That's it. We need to hit them in the head. That works."

He shouted, "Shoot them in the head!! Shoot them in the head!!" But his men couldn't hear over their own shooting. Just seconds later, the first of those things crested the concrete traffic barricades and came crashing down amongst his men. The major used his own M4 assault rifle to pick off several of those beasts that were even then tearing at some of his men.

These weren't human beings they were fighting. They were something more preternatural and raw. They attacked primarily with their teeth, using them like predatory cats to latch onto and then tear at their victims.

Again he shouted, "The head!!!! Shoot them in the head!!!!"

Some of his men heard him this time, but it was too late. Soldiers were being dragged down to the ground by two and three of the creatures at a time. The major started to shoot the machine-gun again until he fired all the rounds into the crowd. Another Humvee from the opposite end of the barricade was already overwhelmed by the things and the Stryker vehicles were wrong facing to make a quick retreat, their open rear doors presenting a very tempting opportunity to several of the beasts. The soldiers inside were trapped and easy prey.

Several of his men broke free from the roadblock and ran toward the major's Humvee; his vehicle now representing the only real way out of the melee. There were six of them. They moved coolly if abruptly. Three would shoot while three moved and then they would alternate. The trained soldiers fired conservatively, trying to save their precious ammunition. The major tried to add some degree of support with his own rifle while he remained in the gunner's position of the Humvee.

The six men were only a few feet from the vehicle when one of their number stumbled and fell behind. The other five continued to fire rounds into the closing mob, but they could not protect their fallen. He was overwhelmed, screaming and kicking, his rifle continuing to fire erratically as his legs and torso were viciously assailed...bitten, ripped, chewed, and devoured.

The crowd's momentary distraction with their latest victim allowed the other soldiers time to retreat to the still idling Humvee and make their escape. No one said a word as they headed for the bridge.

If the engineers had already destroyed the bridge, the sergeant driving the armored sport utility vehicle decided that he would just drive the vehicle as fast as he could off the ledge and hope for a soft water landing from which they could all swim to safety. There was no way in hell that he was going to go down like all those other poor saps back at the roadblock. He'd put a bullet in his brainpan before he'd let that happen.

34.

No rest for the weary. That was a phrase she'd heard batted around the handful of offices at which she had worked. It could be heard on Monday mornings when co-workers attempted to unhappily shake off the lingering effects of the weekend, or when a reporting time deadline threatened to pass without the successful completion of the assigned work.

No rest for the weary...none of them, not a one, had any clue about weariness or exhaustion. For them, it was just about inconvenience and a fleeting sensation that would pass soon enough. There was always the possibility of naps or just slowing down for the day or even finding a delicious double mocha with whipped cream and chocolate sprinkles to chase away the malaise. There was always something on which you could count.

Emma now had an unfortunately firm appreciation for the gravity of the "no rest" sentiment. She couldn't remember ever having felt this tired; not even during her short stint of all-nighters while she enjoyed her even shorter stint in college. Maybe it was because, back then, it wasn't a matter of life and death.

As it was, she hadn't really slept for two solid nights and then had been on the run nonstop during the day. She wondered if this was how it was for prey species such as wildebeests, but then she felt a certain resentment for her animal kingdom example when she realized that even those creatures were granted slight respites for rest and eating.

And that was the other nagging distraction. She was hungry. She didn't just need a snack or trip to a McDonald's for a quick bite. She hadn't had anything other than water for a couple of days and her moaning, acid-churning stomach was in full revolt.

She realized after several more minutes that her eyes were indeed open and that she had been staring, absently, at the crude ceiling of simple, unfinished lumber over her. They weren't, after all, staying at the Captain Cook Hotel or some other establishment that prided itself on its refinements. The three of them, hunted fugitives in their own city, had taken a hasty refuge in a child's tree house for the simple reasons that it was up off the ground and the rope ladder could be and was retracted into the structure, rendering them all but unreachable by any would-be assailants. Once inside, their heart rates could slow slightly and their breathing could relax to a more normal level.

There was at least a fleeting sense of security up off the ground. The comfort was at least enough for them to collect themselves. It was anything but rest; in fact, she felt more tired now than she did before. Her adrenaline had faded from her blood stream and her fatigue was beginning to blunt her senses.

As she stared, she noticed that the boards comprising the ceiling were damp with moisture. At about the same moment, the fact that her exhaled breath was forming a warm, misty cloud immediately in front of her face suddenly occurred to her.

She tried to wrap herself tighter into the very limited warmth of the threadbare blanket that previously served as a floor cover of sorts in the tree house. As cold as she felt, she just knew that it would be unbearable without the minimal warmth the blanket provided.

The moment, despite the cold, was almost serene; provided, of course, that she forgot about the fact that she could possibly be in the midst of Armageddon on a truly Biblical scale.

Quietly, almost silently, tears again pooled in her eyes and rolled down the sides of her face. She wasn't sure why she was crying again. At first, other than the tightness in her chest, she wasn't even certain that she was crying. And when she did understand and accept that she was surrendering to her emotions, she realized that there wasn't a shortage of things about which she could cry.

She didn't fight the tears, fearing it would only lead to the inevitable sobbing. She didn't want any attention, regardless of how well meaning it would be. Maybe one good cry in the morning would suffice for the entire day.

Dr. Caldwell, lying next to her and sharing the blanket, stirred slightly and began to breathe in short, shallow breaths. Another nightmare she figured. At one point during the night, he was almost whimpering. She wondered to herself if his nightmare came close to comparing with the hell they had been enduring for the past two days.

She looked more closely at the man who was, for all intents and purposes, sharing a bed with her. He had a kind, knowing face with shallow lines of experience cut into the skin near his eyes. His hair was a patchy salt and pepper, primarily comprised of pepper. The dark hair growing in on his cheeks, chin, and neck was even and had the appearance of having been manicured, though she realized that it couldn't have been.

She placed her hand lightly on his shoulder to comfort him while not waking him. She made a motion to lie her head back down and snuggle closer against the doctor when she felt the unmistakable sensation that she was being watched. The feeling slithered up her spine like a cold serpent. She looked up and saw Officer Malachi Ivanoff looking directly at her.

Trying to ignore him and act as if she hadn't noticed his staring, she cautiously watched him from the corner of her eyes. At first what she thought she was seeing was anger or possibly betrayal but then, looking through her bangs, she could have sworn that his eyes were actually filled with hunger or possibly lust. As a woman, she had seen that leer in the eyes of men at bars and parties, after alcohol had started the blunting effect on better judgment. Perhaps she was just imagining it, but she was utterly unsettled by it.

She laid her head back down but didn't dare close her eyes. She waited a few seconds, trying to control her breathing. Feigning adjusting her position to find the elusive comfort on the bare planks of the floor, she chanced a glance over the doctor's neck. The officer was apparently asleep again. Maybe he'd been asleep all along and she was just imagining it, but she couldn't shake the unsettling feeling.

No rest for the weary...

35.

Anchorage was quiet; as quiet as the grave. There was no longer any shooting. There were no longer any echoing screams followed by the rush of desperate footsteps. An uneasy peace had settled over the city.

That's not to say that there was no activity within the city's limits. A group of nine of the fiends, separated from the majority of the seemingly aimless specters wandering the city, was slowly meandering in a dead end residential housing court, one way in and one way out on the road. The miserable cold and grey sky very nearly perfectly matched the demons' skin. Once seething and glimmering red, the horrible wounds that once claimed the lives of the human beings that once inhabited the same skin were now soft and brown and malodorous. If the things wore clothing, most of it was in tattered rags; the remnants of a tie and a sport coat, the last clinging strips of a pink velour exercise suit, brown Carhart coveralls stained a deep rust from top to bottom.

Their limbs and heads seemingly rippled with an electric current that pulsed through them as regular as a heartbeat. Every movement they made, however small, carried with it a slight tremble, like coiled springs trying in vain to contain their suppressed but eager energy.

They were searching...searching for the one thing that called to them...searching for their own Sirens. Their heightened predatory senses told them that there was prey near to them. In their own stiff jerked way, each of them raised a nose every few steps. The intoxicating scent of meat...of soft, salty flesh and firm, aromatic blood basted muscle and the delicate, bitter sweetness of the delicious organs...all of it called to them...bade them to wait and to hunger.

"Are they still out there?"

Jerry, peeking through the edge of the curtains, nodded and sighed.

Neil felt the same way and there was no denying it. He wished he could be more confident at least outwardly so or able to mask his disappointment in front of Meghan. He just wasn't a hero, at least in the classic sense of the term. He wasn't capable of being perpetually upbeat and positive. He didn't have superhuman strength, extra sensory perception, and he wasn't a genius. Many people would refer to him as broken or damaged. He wouldn't necessarily agree with that quick assessment. He would probably argue that he was just not interested anymore. That was probably the main reason why he hadn't ever spoken to the beautiful Lani in his building. He just wanted to avoid the disappointment and the heartache that caring about something, about another person, or about himself would ultimately bring.

He wasn't a pessimist for the simple reason that it required more effort than he was willing to put forth. His expectation about life had just been irretrievably altered since his divorce.

He noticed a low but steady hum that tickled the air with its sound vibrations. The noise was annoying and all but impossible to ignore.

"What is that noise? Can everyone hear it or is it just my ears?"

Tony stood up and walked back into the dining room. "No, we can all hear it alright and it's starting to get on my nerves."

Jerry continued the thought, "I think that the hum has been there all along but there needed to be enough of them there for us to hear them."

"How many now?"

"Nine and I think there are some more coming this direction from the road."

Tony turned as he made his way down the narrow kitchen and asked, "Now there are nine?"

"Yeah, and more to come. I think the moaning is working as a kind of beacon for others."

Rachel reeled back in her recliner and asked, "What the fuck did you just say? Sorry kids."

Meghan answered, "It's okay. They're back in the bedroom sleeping."

"Okay, then what the fuck did you just say?"

As usual, Jerry hesitated before he began. It was just difficult for him to commit himself to anything. Sticking his neck out in the past had gotten him nothing but trouble. And he wasn't an expert. Just because he'd played some games, watched some movies, and read some books didn't mean that he was some fucking Dr. Van Helsing of zombies. He was just a kid and wanted to go back to that. He always did. He missed not having to make decisions, or at least not having to be held terribly accountable for those decisions. "I'm guessing that the noise has been there all along. It was probably just subsonic because there weren't enough of them yet. Or maybe it's because the city is quieter. Whatever. It doesn't really resemble a sound that I could place. It's not really a sound at all. It's more like a vibration than it is a sound. Can everyone else feel it?"

Meghan nodded her head, "Yeah, I think you're right. It's actually nauseating me a little." she leaned toward Neil and rested against him. Tentatively, slowly, he raised his hand and wrapped it around her shoulders. She nestled into him in search of comfort.

"Well," he continued, "the vibrations were probably always there, it just took more of them to become powerful enough for our ears to detect it."

Tony asked, already suspecting the answer, "Our ears? Aren't they just us?"

"Yeah, but they died and came back and all the result of some kind of virus or some other highly transmittable organism. Who knows what all changes took place as a result of the infection. I think it is safe to assume that their senses are all heightened."

Kim, coming from the dining room where she had been a silent participant in the conversation thus far, asked, "Why do you say that?"

"Well, they're predators now in a more primal and animalistic sense. They're hunters and hunter species have long relied on their senses to detect, track, and ultimately kill their prey."

Soberly, Meghan said, "Us."

Neil asked the room, "What are we gonna do?"

Rachel, virtually melted to the fabric of her recliner so far she was sunken into the chair, answered, "Why the hell are you asking us? You're the guy who's had the answers all along. You tell us. What are we going to do?"

"I don't know for sure Rachel. I'm new at this too. I guess for the time being we just wait and see. We can afford to stall and not rush into things. Maybe time will work to our advantage."

"And what do you mean by that?"

Looking up at him and smiling, Meghan asked, "Yeah, what's runnin' through that head of yours?"

Neil guided Meghan back into a standing position and stepped away for a second. "These things. They're just dead bodies, right? Well, dead bodies rot, right? They decompose. Ashes to ashes and dust to dust. Maybe as that starts to happen, these things will start to slow down or give us some other sort of advantage. Maybe as their muscle tissue becomes tighter with water loss they'll slow down. Maybe they'll start acting like the zombies in the Romero movies. They were slow and usually overwhelmed victims through sheer numbers."

Jerry interjected, "Yeah, you may be right. I guess I hope you're right. I wonder how long until desiccation begins to take its toll. Do you think that their...um...feeding impacts the process?"

Rachel interrupted the discussion with a very direct, "What the fuck does it matter? You're not gettin' my ass back out there. And if the rest of you are smart, you'd just stay hidden too."

She started to cry, which forced her words out in sputtering starts and stops. "I mean...does...does...any of...th-th-that even matter? Is...is this Armageddon?" The last word spilled from her lips and made its way through the room like a shadow, darkening as it crept.

She looked up from the floor and let the tears course down her cheeks. Her eyes were swollen and her cheeks were red and splotchy. She looked at Neil and asked, "Is this really the end of the world like in The Bible?"

Typically in the past, to hear a question like that, one had to be walking in downtown San Francisco or some other larger than life metropolis and the asker would be wearing a large cardboard sign written in scrawled marker with a date for the end of the world. It wasn't a question that normally arose in casual conversation. Neil read a story a long time ago in which everyone on Earth knew that the end of the world was happening that night after everyone was asleep. Even with that knowledge, the entire population simply went to sleep like normal, to never wake again. That was really the first time he had truly contemplated the end of existence. He read the story in a college class. The discussion that followed culminated in an examination of what each of them would do today if they knew that tomorrow would never come.

And now here it was; a very real possibility that he was living that exact scenario. He thought to himself, ain't life a bitch. I've actually met someone that it feels so natural to connect with so well so quickly and time has run out. He looked at her. He knew that everyone in the room was looking at him again, but he didn't care. He needed to know if he was just imagining the energy between them. Maybe he was just creating the illusion to comfort his mind. When he looked in her eyes though, he realized it didn't really matter because she was looking at him and her eyes were kind and warm and comfortable.

If it was the end of the world, he couldn't think of a better feeling to have when it all shook down. He didn't feel the need to answer Rachel immediately. He did, however, look away from Meghan and felt better than he had in a long time.

Meghan looked over at Rachel and said, "I'm not necessarily saying that I even believe in that line of thinking, but, regardless, I'm not goin' down without a fight. Don't expect me to pray for salvation and ditch on this world. I say let's figure a way outta this. If we wait, then we wait. And if we need to figure out when and how to boogey, well I'm down with that too. We just all need to keep talkin' and thinkin' and watchin' out for one another."

Neil interrupted, "First things first. It feels a little cool in here today."

Tony, still in the dining room, said, "Yeah, the turtle thermostat hanging on the window here says that it's only fifty degrees outside."

"And it's only gonna get cooler."

"Whatdawe do?"

Neil didn't know. If they were to survive, they needed to

stay warm. But they also couldn't risk detection by those things.

To the room, but more specifically to Jerry, he asked, "Do ya think that smoke from a fire would give us away?"

Tony, with a smile on his face, jokingly said, "Maybe if ours isn't the only fire, then ..."

Meghan and Kim both looked at him and said in unison, "Huh?"

"Well, I'm a bit of a pyro and if it would help I might be willing to venture out and start us a fire down the road a bit."

Kim demanded, "Are you outta your fucking mind!"

"C-mon Kim. You know how much of a pyro I am. Here's my big chance to start a real fire and not get in trouble for it...hell, even be encouraged to set it. You tellin' me that you want me to pass that kind of an opportunity by?"

"Yeah, but that doesn't mean ya gotta get yourself killed to satisfy your fetish. 'Sides, we don't even know if this is gonna work."

"Relax, I'll be safe. It's not like I wanna die or anything."

Neil, with that comment, was suddenly reminded of the facetious rule that he would demand be followed in athletic contests, however mundane they may have been. No one is allowed to die was the largely comedic rule that all at once became much more profound. The words, as bright and buzzing as neon, flashed in his head, threatening to become a motivational mantra.

Ignoring the neon, Neil said, "She's right Tony. This isn't worth getting yourself killed over. We can probably think of something else. This was really only going to buy us some time anyway and that was only if it worked."

"If I thought I could actually end up dead doing this, d'ya think that I'd be volunteering?"

Kim started to speak, but thought better of it and went back into the bedroom in which Jules and Danny were still sleeping.

With his hands pressed tightly together in front of himself, Neil began, "Okay, let's come up with a plan then. Any ideas?"

36.

Crouched and moving with as much speed as stealth would allow, Neil made it to the storage shed in the back of the yard. Just as Jerry had said, there was a grass caked red lawnmower. He looked around in the obscuring darkness and finally found it. He grabbed the metal handle on the gas can and was relieved to find that it was mostly full. Lugging it back to Tony, waiting by the six-foot privacy fence separating this yard from the next one, he tried not to cause the flammable liquid to slosh too much. But like a fart in church, he imagined that everyone and everything in the vicinity could hear it.

Arriving, he asked, "Okay, we ready to go?"

Tony nodded and smiled. They both looked up at Jerry standing at the ready on the deck behind them. From his vantage point, he could pretty well see into all the yards around them. He lifted the scoped hunting rifle above his head as he had seen soldiers do in World War II movies. Without lowering the rifle, he gave them a thumbs up signal and waved them over.

Meghan was there with Jerry as well. She waved to Neil and then blew him a kiss. She looked over them and into the yard to which they were heading. It was still empty, or at least it appeared empty. She couldn't see the spaces close to the fence, the far side of the yard behind the shed and full tree, and, of course, the shadows in the house were a terrifying possibility to all of them. She didn't see Neil and Tony go over the fence. She did, however, see both sets of hands come to the top of the fence and pull the ladder over.

37.

Reaching up to pull the ladder from the fence, Neil all but involuntarily withdrew his hands as if he had been burned. The cocktail of adrenaline and fear was forcing his hands into shaking fits that could rival a Parkinson tic. He was afraid that he might rattle the metal parts of their fence-scaling ladder they'd found hanging on the inside wall of the garage. They couldn't afford the attention that such noise might bring.

Tony, looking out into the new yard whispered, "I'm scared shitless."

Neil's heart was threatening to use his throat as an expressway as it made its way up and out his mouth. He swallowed cautiously, not wanting to tempt fate. At the back of his throat, a not too subtle pungence arose and settled in his mouth...the flavor of fear.

Neil whispered, "Speed. The quicker we get in, the quicker we get out. I don't know about you, but I want to be back in our house as quick as we can."

"I'm with you boss."

They started to run, one at each end of the ladder. The yard they were in, they realized, was not entirely enclosed. There were only fences on three sides, the front open to the street. They both stopped, looked at the empty street in front of the house, looked at one another, and decided to finish the job anyway. The absence of any of those things, helped to embolden their resolve.

Tony clamored over the ladder and Neil quickly followed. This was the yard and this was the house. There was a big pile of firewood stacked against the back wall of the house. Without even seeing his face, Neil could feel Tony's delightful smile.

38.

Meghan looked over at Jerry when she saw the smoke coming from two houses over. In another life, seeing smoke would have had her running to the telephone to call the fire department. It would have drawn a crowd of concerned neighbors to the street. It would have normally solicited a response other than relief and hope. Jerry's own facial expression mirrored hers.

She looked past him, hoping to see Neil coming over the fence. "Oh shit!"

Jerry started to ask but then looked for himself. One of the ghouls, what appeared to be a former grocery clerk, was stumbling into the backyard that was between Neil and Tony and themselves. Its left leg was obviously broken and partially missing. It hopped on its good leg and used the damaged limb to balance itself precariously between jumps. Like a movie mummy's tattered linen rags, the fiend's shredded clothing hung from it, swaying with each uneven movement.

Like stone golems, Jerry and Meghan froze. Neither knew if the thing recognized them for what they were. Was it scent or movement that attracted the attention? Jerry had wondered to himself if the zombies might be able to detect heat signatures using an animalistic form of infrared. Bats used a sophisticated but natural form of sonar to navigate the blackness of night. Who's to say that the infection that caused reanimation didn't alter the senses in the process? As the past few days had taught all of them, nothing was beyond the realm of possibilities anymore.

At first it didn't appear that the beast could see them. They could tell that he saw something that caught his eye, but were relatively certain that his primal brain still hadn't sorted it all out. His eyes were transfixed on them though.

And then Tony was coming over the fence in a hurry. He very nearly ran into the former grocery clerk, who all but spun on his one good limb like a deranged music box ballerina. It lost its balance, as did Tony, and fell to the ground. The two scrambled, each in his own way, back to their feet. Neil, in the meantime, was cresting the fence and coming down in the midst of the struggle. He realized the possibility of what was unfolding before he saw the fiend.

"Fuuuuuuuck!" Neil shouted as he landed.

The thing turned and faced Neil, whose spine seized with fear instantly. Try as he might, he couldn't lift his feet or even his arms. He was as stuck as a fly in a web. He felt just as vulnerable and helpless as well. He couldn't swallow. He could barely draw a breath.

The creature's smell was as intimidating as its appearance; neither of which was anything short of frightening. The putrescent dark wounds on its neck near its ear and its now shattered leg colored the air all around it with the sickening rotten smell that typically accompanied the early spring or fall; that smell of fresh death and decay stewing in the fermenting broth of the latest rain or heavy dew...only this odor was magnified a hundred times. Relentlessly churning the acid collecting therein, Neil's stomach began to make audible sucking sounds.

It reached out for Neil, who only then realized that on its left hand were only two fingers; the others having been gnawed down to below the first knuckle. A further chill then roughly handled Neil's immobile spine. He couldn't move. He could only watch. He was a spectator at his own death.

Its hands grabbed hold of Neil's jacket and tried to pull him closer to its chomping jaws. Neil's arms somehow broke free of their paralysis and grabbed hold of his attacker's ragged smock in an attempt to hold him at bay. Looking like a pair of tussling hockey players, they shifted positions slightly and moments later it was over.

Neil let go and the beast's lifeless body fell at his feet. The thing's head was all but gone from about the ear up. Neil saw Tony who was pointing up at Jerry on the deck. He still had the hunting rifle on his shoulder at the ready. Neil waved to him thankfully and looked back down at the purulent pile of flesh. It was hard to remember that it was at one time a man...a young man, not much more than a teen really.

With a slap to his shoulder, Tony exhorted Neil, "C-mon goddamnit. Can't you hear that?"

Neil shook the daze and focused on it. It was the sound of hundreds of footsteps on pavement and the sound was growing as its source grew nearer. Neil nodded and they both ran off, carrying the ladder haphazardly and leaning it against the fence again without the same care or caution exercised in their coming. With adrenaline-amplified muscles, the two of them were able to negotiate the six-foot high cedar fence fairly easily, hardly even using the ladder to crest the wooden barrier. When Neil came down on the opposite side, he felt a sense of relief and wonderment overtake him. He and Tony grabbed the metal top of their climbing aid and pulled it over, letting it rattle and crash just inside their side of the fence.

Despite the fact that the back deck on which Meghan and Jerry were still standing was missing its bottom several steps, a cautionary move suggested by Jerry earlier, Tony and Neil were able to get themselves up and out of the yard without even slowing their pace. Like seasoned gymnasts, they leapt up and were on the deck in a matter of seconds.

"Are we good?" asked Jerry.

With shaking hands and a spine that was still twitching and tingling with fear and adrenaline, Neil said, "Let's just get back inside."

39.

Back in the living room of their house-turned-bunker, Neil was finding it hard to catch his breath. He couldn't shake the hold from his mind of the creature's face and its cold dead eyes, the eyes of a predator...of a shark, not a man. There wasn't a shred of humanity in him at all. He wasn't even quite sure if it was even fitting to be referring to it as he or him.

Meghan put her hand on his shoulder and started to rub him in gentle circles. When he looked up at her though she realized that he wasn't even aware that she was touching him. He pulled away abruptly and walked over to the window. He looked through the crack in the blind down the street toward the now burning house. It seemed to be working. All of them that were in the street were starting to drift toward the fire. There were perhaps fifty of them by then. Every time he happened to look out into the street, there seemed to be more. Soon the house would be as much a prison as a sanctuary. How much longer could they hold out?

He needed a distraction. "Hey Tony. How about a repeat performance but on a much smaller scale?" Neil pointed to the fireplace and nodded.

Tony, who had been close to mauled by the very relieved and emotional Kim, pulled himself away and nodded. "Yeah. Good idea. Let's get this place a little warmer. Figure we earned it."

With a sarcastic bark, Neil answered, "Yeah," and continued to chuckle uncomfortably.

"I figure that's the last time we're gonna be doin' that, huh?"

Neil nodded but couldn't hide the pools gathering in the corners of his eyes. He shook his head but couldn't speak at first.

With Meghan again at his side and with her arm around his shoulders, he exhaled a long, stilted breath and said with an equally uncomfortable and forced smile, "Like chef said,...'never get off the boat. Never.' You might just run into a tiger like he did."

The comment and the joke were lost on everyone except Jerry who'd actually seen <u>Apocalypse Now</u>. He thought to himself that staying on the boat, regardless of what boat it was, always seemed to be a great idea but it very rarely worked out that way. There was always something out there that lured you or scared you off the boat. And then the jungle would eat your soul.

40.

"I don't see any of them. I think it's okay."

"Look again. Just make sure. I don't wanna get down and..."

Dr. Caldwell nodded and leaned down for another peek. The yard appeared to be empty. He moved himself so that he could get a three hundred and sixty degree look and still didn't see anything.

He didn't look back this time, but decided just to drop himself down. He stepped behind the tree in which the tree fort was sitting. He looked up into the trapdoor opening on the bottom of their sanctuary. He nodded to Emma and signaled with his hand to join him, which she did with Officer Ivanoff following quickly on her heels.

Just looking around at what was once a friendly suburban backyard and the scene of games, fun, and laughter and knowing that at every corner and behind every door possibly lurked unimaginable horrors, Dr. Caldwell felt his breath catch in the back of his throat. Nothing was nor would it ever be the same again.

Emma's stomach begged for food with an audible sucking and churning sound. "I could really use a Danish and a mocha Grande right about now."

Officer Ivanoff said, "Fat chance of that."

Staring intently at the back door of the house in whose backyard they were standing, Dr. Caldwell said, "She might have a point. It seems to be quiet and we don't know when we might

179

get another chance to eat. Maybe we should check out what's inside."

"D'ya think it's safe?" asked the doubtful police officer.

"I don't know, but how long can we possibly last with no food in our bellies? This part of town seems to be deserted, thankfully. Maybe our absent hosts have some food in there for us."

"And if one of those things is in there?"

Emma looked at the doctor wondering about his response as well. He held up the large silver revolver and said, "I guess if you guys hear this thing go off, you better get running. And here," the doctor handed the water bottle he had been carrying in his jacket pocket to Emma. "Just in case."

With that, walking like a bad actor in an even worse police crime drama, the doctor made his way across the yard and went into the unlocked back door. He disappeared for a few seconds but reappeared unmolested much to Emma's and Malachi's relief.

"C-mon. There's food upstairs still on the kitchen counters. Like they knew to expect us."

Emma shuddered to herself at the thought of what that meant. A few of days ago, some ordinary family was rising early with the day. They were probably getting lunches together for later and talking about their day when they heard the news of the mayhem. They probably flew out the door, never looking back at the partially finished lunches or the ordinary lives that they were leaving behind forever.

Once inside, she looked around and further fleshed out the images in her mind. There were children's toys, both boy and girl, scattered here and there. Next to the now crusty sandwiches in mid-preparation sat Star Wars and Barbie lunch boxes.

Dr. Caldwell pulled a tab on the top of a can of fruit cocktail and emptied the contents into his mouth and onto his cheeks. He chomped the chunks of peaches, pears, grapes, and cherries in grand style. From the non-functioning and stale refrigerator, he produced a bottle of still cool orange soda and sucked it down greedily straight from the bottle. He belched loudly and handed the two-liter bottle to the police officer. Office Ivanoff was chewing a granola cereal bar and eagerly drank from the soda bottle. He went to the window that looked out over the front yard and the street beyond.

He turned around and asked sourly, "So, you want the good news or the bad news?"

Emma said defiantly, "Can't it wait until I at least have a full stomach? I don't think marshmallows have ever tasted this good."

"Whatever you say, your majesty."

"If I wasn't having such a good time eating, I'd tell you to go fuck yourself, but you're gonna have to do that for me. I'm not that interested in dealing with you right at this moment."

Stung, the police officer said, "You know, under different circumstances..."

With a little sass she asked, "What? We 'coulda been friends or something."

"No. Hell no. Under different circumstances, you'd never be allowed to speak to me like that."

"You know, that shit may fly out in the Bush, but you can plain forget about it with me. Got it?" declared Emma, not once slowing her chewing as she tossed in mini-marshmallows one after the other.

Dr. Caldwell, still hung up on the good news and bad news, asked calmly, "Officer, I'd like to hear both the good and the bad news."

"Well, the good news is that I think we're safe for the moment and I don't think they know that we're here."

"They?"

"Yeah, that's the bad news. There's a crowd of those things out in the street. They just look like they're waiting for something."

"Waiting for something?" asked the doctor.

And Emma shared all of their thoughts, "Yeah, waiting for us to fuck up and become dinner."

The doctor, shaking his head and half-heartedly chuckling, said, "You sure got a way of cutting to the chase of things don't you."

"It's a gift. What can I say?"

Sneering as he left the room, Officer Ivanoff said, "Some gift. Too bad..." His words trailed off as he made his way down the hallway.

Dr. Caldwell, realizing where the police officer was heading, said in a rush, "Officer, I haven't been in any of those rooms yet."

"Yeah?"

"Meaning, I don't know what's on the other side of any of those doors."

The police officer's hand stopped abruptly, just inches from a doorknob. The hand, with a mind and an instinct all its own, fell to his side and pulled the 9mm pistol from its hip holster. The cool oily metal of the pistol grip was comforting. The lingering tingles of fear that had sought refuge in the hand's fingertips lost their grip and quickly faded.

With his gun raised and in a firing stance, Officer Malachi backed out of the hallway and back into the main room. "You didn't think to check it all out first?"

"I listened at each door and didn't hear anything. The house seems abandoned, but..."

Finishing his thought, "But you didn't see fit to check it all out before inviting us in."

Interjecting herself into the conversation, "Hey, he hasn't been trained in any of this. Would you have done any better?"

"I would have at least checked the whole place out first."

"As I recall, you weren't exactly jumping to come in here in the first place. At least the doc here got us in."

Walking down the hall, she continued, "And if neither of you have the balls to check the place out, then I guess it's just up to me." As she finished the last sentence, she flew open the first door to reveal a coat closet doing its best to contain all the contents of its overstuffed space. The long handle of a tilted floor vacuum cleaner slowly fell and caused each of their hearts to skip a beat. Emma plastered herself to the opposite wall trying to avoid the slow reach. When she opened her eyes again and realized her error, she said, "Okay, I think I just wet myself."

Dr. Caldwell demanded, "What in the hell were you thinking?"

"I don't know. I think it was just a sugar buzz from all of those marshmallows. Maybe we should open the other doors together."

"Yeah, I think you may be right."

Officer Malachi Ivanoff went back over to the front window to keep an eye on the ghouls in the street. It appeared that they were in yet another cul de sac of the same ghost town. He looked out onto the same scene that he'd seen several times before. Some of the houses' front doors were still open as were most of the garage doors. There were clothes and toys in all of the yards along with discarded luggage and family heirlooms. When all was said and done, none of that mattered anymore. It was all about the escape. He wondered how many of those that tried, were actually able to get away. He wasn't quite sure how that made him feel.

Pondering his luck, his resourcefulness, and his mortality, he looked down the street and saw the smoke and then the flames. There was a house on the opposite side of the street and then about a half a block away that was burning. The fire was actually attracting most of those beasts to it. That was, in Officer Ivanoff's opinion, the happiest coincidence they had encountered yet. The noise and the smoke should be a good distraction for them when they decided to make a move.

41.

The downstairs of their new accommodations was largely all garage and virtually no windows. There was the backdoor through which they had entered that had to be secured and then there was a small window in the utility room. That window was too tight to admit everything but the smallest of assailants. Even so, figuring that they weren't going to be checking the hot water heater or doing any laundry, Dr. Caldwell figured they would just need to seal that room.

Officer Ivanoff used a scavenged hammer and screwdriver to remove a door from its hinges from one of the empty bedroom upstairs. Dr. Caldwell and Emma then nailed the door across the door and window of the backdoor. To lessen the volume of hammering, the doctor laid some cloth over the nails. They worked as quietly as they could.

After a handful of hours, the house felt secure if a little cold and they could all relax a little.

Emma went to the front window and peered through. She felt that spectator-at-the-scene-of-an-accident urge overcome her as she watched the beasts in the street. Their movements seemed stiffer now, more robotic and less organic. Their appearance, though, was still nightmarish and enough to freeze her in her tracks if she wasn't careful. She counted at least thirty of them loitering in the street and knew that there were more out of sight down the road further.

The fire down the road seemed to be close to running its course. The house in which the fire was currently residing was all but burned by then. She looked closer at the house next to it to make sure that the fire was not spreading. She couldn't be certain, but it didn't appear that the fire had reached across the privacy fence separating the two properties.

She looked to the next house down the line and didn't see any indication of fire either until she looked up at its roof. She about fell over she was so surprised and excited. She looked into the room at Dr. Caldwell and, without uttering a word, looked back out to make certain that her eyes were not deceiving her. From the chimney atop the roof, smoke was meandering its way up and out toward the clouds. She tried to determine if there was any other sign of fire. No, it just appeared that the fireplace had a fire in it. And if there was a fire in the fireplace, then it just stood to reason that there were people inside.

"Doc, I think there are more than just us and those things here on this block."

Trying to dial in a faint signal on a battery powered radio, the doctor looked up and asked what she meant.

"I think there might be people over in that house across the street from us."

"Why do you think that?" asked a disbelieving Malachi Ivanoff, emerging from the kitchen.

"Well, the bottom windows are boarded up and I see smoke coming from the fire place."

"Probably just smoke that drifted over the house from the fire down the way. You're just seeing what you want to see."

The doctor, now standing next to Emma and looking out the window, said, "No, Mal. She may be on to something. The wind is blowing the smoke in the opposite direction. I think I do see smoke coming from the chimney."

"It could just be a smoldering fire from a wood burning stove."

"Yeah and it could be the only other survivors that we've encountered since this whole thing began. Doesn't that excite you in the slightest."

"Even if there are people over there, what does it matter?"

Emma, stupefied by the police officer's attitude, asked, "What does it matter? Those are other people over there possibly. Maybe they've got news or have some of this figured out."

"And what good does it do us? Even if there is somebody over there, how do we talk to them? With those things between us and them, they might as well be on the other side of the Cook Inlet."

The doctor, not wanting to let something as elusive as hope get away, added, "Yeah, but that's a problem that can be dealt with. I don't want to rush into anything, but if we keep an eye across the street, maybe...just maybe we can determine if there is indeed someone there. Once we've done that, it's just a matter of figuring the safest way to get over there."

"Thank you Doc. I was afraid that I was all alone on this one."

"None of us are alone in anything. We do everything together."

42.

"Favorite movie of all time? Hmmmm. The problem with that question is that there are so many favorites out there. It's like asking your favorite song, ya know. It kind of depends on your mood."

Jerry, shaking his head, demanded with a smile, "Nope. Not again. You're not gonna weasel yourself out of answering."

Mouth agape in mock disgust, Neil said, "Again. What do you mean again? When have I weaseled...?"

"What about right now? You're stalling. I'm calling your bluff. C-mon."

"Favorite movie? Damn. I really like movies. When I just closed my eyes, the title that came to me was The Usual Suspects,"

Meghan asked, "What else, Mr. Movieman?"

"What genre?"

Jerry fired off, "Comedy."

"Classic or Modern?"

"Ooooooh, specific. Both."

"I really like Bringing Up Baby with Hepburn and Grant. The first time I saw it was with my dad at my grandparents' house. We were sitting at the kitchen table and watching it while Grandma cooked and smoked. Back when people still smoked in their houses. I remember hearing my dad laughing out in the kitchen, so I wandered in to check out what was so funny. He had one of those laughs you know. You just had to find out what could solicit such laughter. So I sat down and just started watching. Kate

189

Hepburn was just so funny and sweet. Ya know? And Grant. He was such a good straight man. D'ya remember him in <u>Arsenic and Old Lace</u>?" He trailed off in the past.

Meghan was thinking to herself that she may just love this guy but decided to distract herself and the conversation with, "And modern?"

The memory hadn't completely faded...was stalling there on the periphery, teasing. He thought a moment longer and then looked at Meghan and said, "Maybe <u>Wonder Boys</u>."

Meghan asked, surprised, "<u>Wonder Boys</u>? That's a comedy?"

"What's wrong with that?"

"Well, when I think about ha-ha comedies, <u>Wonder Boys</u> isn't one that comes to mind?"

"Well what would say then?"

"What about <u>Uncle Buck</u>?"

"I can live with that."

Jerry said, "But <u>Wonder Boys </u>is a hell of a movie. One of Douglas' best."

Meghan still persisted, "But a comedy?"

Defending himself now, Neil said, "In the classic sense of a comedy, yes it is. Everyone wins and the hero gets the girl and all of the action and dialogue is humorous, light and somewhat lyrical."

Giggling, Meghan teased, "Listen to you. 'Light and lyrical.' Why is it that you weren't teaching or something?"

"What could I possibly be qualified to teach?"

Jerry said somberly, "Apocalypse Survival 101."

They all nodded slowly, reluctantly. Neil was still nodding when he asked, "Uncle Buck huh?"

"Yeah and what's wrong with that?" and Meghan's hands slid to her hips in defiant protest.

"I wasn't suggesting there was anything wrong with..."

Abruptly closing the distance between him and her until she was all but pushing him over, Meghan playfully threatened, "That's right you weren't suggesting. If you know what's good for you anyway."

Like a good boxing referee, Jerry separated the two and sent each of them to their corners.

Neil, as a way of perhaps mock appeasement, said, "<u>Uncle Buck </u>is Candy at his best."

Jerry added, "I was just a little kid when John Candy kicked it but I remember it. He was a funny guy that's for sure."

Not wanting the game to stop, Jerry asked, "Okay, what about other movies? I love talking movies."

"You do it often?" asked Meghan.

"Naw. Not really. Only when I get to hang out with MDs at Providence during the rare down time. Naw. Most of my friends were in to whatever was at the theaters or on the radio right now, ya know. I mean, I'm not trying to suggest that I'm better than them or that I don't on occasion like whatever is right now, but I'm not a slave to seeing or having the latest and greatest of anything. Sometimes the greatest happened a long time before the latest ever came along."

43.

Jules was sleeping peacefully in the bed with pink sheets and flowered pillow cases. The dog, which everyone had taken to calling Lucky, was on the floor next to the bed and sleeping as well. Danny, however, couldn't get himself comfortable enough to sleep. His mind wouldn't stop turning over questions and every time he did close his eyes for longer than a simple blink, he always saw that face from out at the glacier. That was where it had all started. That day seemed so long ago. He wasn't even sure how long ago it was or even what day it was.

He sat up in bed and tried to think about something else. He tried to think about home and his parents. He tried to think about his own dog, a great Golden Retriever named Max, who was, hopefully, waiting for him back home. He even thought about his older sister. He wondered if he'd ever see them again. He was crying before he even realized that the tears were streaming down his cheeks and getting his shirt wet.

He didn't like this one bit. He just wanted to be back at home. He knew deep down that all of these people were looking out for him and Jules, but nothing could take the place of his mother's compassion. Her voice just made everything better for him. He needed her voice and her comfort. She could make everything all right regardless of the situation. He found himself getting upset that he decided to come to Alaska at all. His mom had said that it was up to him whether he went or not. She wasn't going to force him, though she did say that she thought that he might regret it if he didn't. Boy was she wrong.

He wondered if his family was still safe or if the whole world had been turned upside down by what was happening here in Alaska. Was this same thing happening everywhere? Jules stirred slightly and rolled over onto her side. The dog's head rose from the floor to inspect the new noise. Danny caught the dog's attention and motioned for him to join Danny on the bed. The dog hopped up eagerly, obviously a treat that he was not accustomed to enjoying. He circled three or four times before finally plopping himself down heavily next to Danny's leg. Possibly sensing Danny's unease, Lucky laid his head across Danny's thigh and breathed a long, loud sigh. Lucky wasn't Max by a long shot, but he was friendly and seemed to need attention from Danny and Jules. He was quite obviously a child's dog and was missing its human counterpart.

Danny scratched him behind the ears, like he'd seen Jerry do, and then curled up next to him. The dog's breathing, deep and rhythmic, helped to relax Danny enough to let him drift off to sleep. The dog too found his way back to sleep.

44.

"What's up buttercup?"

Kim looked back at her friend Tony who was even then walking down the hallway toward her. "I thought I heard crying or sobbing coming from back here."

"Looks like the kids are still asleep."

"Yeah."

"D-ya think they understand what's going on?"

"God, I hope not. I mean, their family. It all started with them. Can you imagine?"

"No. No way. Who would have even thought this would be happening? I don't even know that I can believe it and I'm living through it. Well, hopefully anyway."

Kim cocked her eyebrow at that comment and answered, "Speaking of which. You've done your hero bit now, right. Can we agree to let the other heroes step up and do their parts now? I don't think I can handle a repeat performance of yesterday. And I know that I can't handle losing you after losing everything else."

"You won't get any arguments from me."

"Tony, is everything going to work out? Are we gonna make it through this alright?"

"If we stick together, I think we've got a better chance than trying to do this alone."

"That's not really much of an answer, ya know."

"What do you want exactly?"

"I want you to tell me that everything is going to be alright and that we're gonna make it through all this and that there's still

195

going to be a world left to live in. Can you do that?"

Tony put his big arms around Kim and pulled her into his chest. She didn't resist even a little. She melted against him and tried to claw even closer. With his cheek resting on the top of her head he said, "I'm not going to let anything happen to you, that's for sure, because I can't imagine a world without you in it."

It wasn't the answer that she wanted, but it would do. Kim, once again, damned her bad luck for having all but fallen in love with yet another man who didn't want to have anything to do with her romantically. She'd loved boys with girlfriends, young men with fiancées, and men with wives. Sometimes there were brief moments of romance, fiery sweet, but all of those relationships had ended the same. And now, she was falling for a gay man. Dumb luck. Pure and simple.

45.

"What's wrong sweetie?" asked Meghan, her blues eyes soft and concerned.

It was later in the day and the house around them was buzzing, albeit quietly, with life and activity. Jerry had found a portable DVD player with a charged battery pack and battery back-up; so he, Jules, Danny, and Rachel were all watching a Pixar movie in the front room. Kim and Tony were trying to scrape together a meal in the kitchen. A Coleman cook stove was busy heating a can of beans while peanut butter and jelly were being slathered on bread. Tony hummed while Kim quietly sang to the tune. It was all just too normal...too routine for Neil to take. He retreated to the garage and, of course, Meghan had followed him.

With the CD player in the minivan melodically making its way through a tune, the two of them continued their conversation. Neil just wanted someone to understand what he was feeling; the discomforting thoughts that just wouldn't give his mind peace.

"I...I...," he looked away trying to hide his shame for the tears forming in the corner of his eyes. He wasn't accustomed to crying. It just wasn't something that he did. And yet, the urge to cry was a feeling that hovered so closely over the past few days that the feeling alone was enough to set him off at a moment's notice. Finding the base root of his emotions, he tried to sum it up with, "I've never been this...scared before."

"Oh, honey," she tried to soothe him with a soft caress on the back of Neil's neck.

He turned back toward her and tried to make her understand, "You didn't see...you couldn't have seen."

"What sweetie?"

"...those eyes. And that smell. It was the most horrific odor that's ever been, I'm sure. It was all the bad smells...rotting fish, decaying plants in the spring, body odor, shit...all of it put together and then made worse. And that sound that it made. It was as much a sensation that I could feel as hear. It rumbled down in the pit of my stomach and rattled my knees. But its eyes...I've never seen anything so empty and soulless but, at the same time, so angry and full of rage. All the fear in the world was there in the blackness."

She nodded and started to speak but thought better of it and chose to let him continue instead.

"We can't stay here indefinitely and I don't think anyone is coming to help us. Hell, there may not be anyone out there anymore anyway. We're running out of options and I am petrified about going back out there again."

"Sweetie, we're all..."

"No! You don't understand. I've never been this afraid of anything...ever. Not even when I was a boy and all things were possible was I this afraid. Back then, I knew that Mom in the next room would always come to rescue me from the Boogie Man in the closet or the monster under the bed. Just knowing that she was there was enough to hold the fear at least partially at bay. I didn't know that fear like this even existed...was even possible."

They were quiet for a few minutes while Jack Johnson on the cd sung about all the pretty people and where they've gone.

Meghan took Neil's hand in hers and asked him, "Are you more afraid of what might happen to you or about making a wrong decision that might lead to something happening to one of us...one of the kids maybe?"

He thought about that for a few seconds. He, at first, was inclined to say that he was terrified about his own well-being. After all, who likes to consider the prospect of being eaten alive? He remembered the curly blonde haired guy in the parking lot of his office building. He could still see the man flailing his hands about wildly trying to fend off his attacker. And then he remembered seeing the man's hands, held in the air uselessly and coming together in weaker and weaker fists as he was disemboweled and eaten. Neil felt true nausea come over him when he imagined Meghan lying there instead. He couldn't picture himself there but seeing Meghan suffer such a fate was too much.

He lowered his head until his cheek rested against Meghan's chest. Her heartbeat was strong and her breaths were deep. He tried to match his own breathing to hers so that he might be able to get control of his own heartbeat.

"I don't know what I'm more afraid of anymore...losing me or losing you."

She hugged him tighter against her, the way that she used to do to her fiancé when life was too much for him to bear on his own. She closed her eyes and let the tears come. They dripped down her cheeks and onto Neil's back. "Oh sweetie, what are we going to do with you? My poor hero."

Jack Johnson's disembodied voice was still asking the world about the good people. The song had a light feel to it, but the question and the frustration were serious and ardent. It was the only sound in the minivan other than their breathing. Neil wondered too where all the people, both good and bad, had gone. He was going through options in his mind when the door from the garage to the house was opened, letting in a slice of light that cut into the darkness surrounding the minivan. It was Jerry.

"Guys. I hate to interrupt, but I think we've got company in one of the houses across the street."

Neil, still feeling exposed and a little defeated, asked, "Yeah? And your point is?"

"I'm talking about people. You know, the live variety and not the kind that wants to have all of us for dinner."

Feeling excited and even a little hopeful, Neil asked, "What?"

"Yeah. I think we...well, Rachel saw someone across the street in one of the houses. And I think that they know that we're here too."

46.

Emma was back at the window again. She was sure that she saw movement at the corner of the drawn blinds in the house across the way. Maybe she was just being hopeful and seeing what she wanted to see as Police Officer Ivanoff had suggested, but she didn't believe that for even an instant. She was wondering if there was a way to get their attention without getting the unwanted attention of those things down on the street between them.

The ghouls, whose numbers had grown over the past several hours, had been gradually making their way down into the cul de sac. They were an impassable barrier...a sea that defied navigation. Emma knew that if there were people over there, then the barrier would have to be addressed. Until then though, she just had to find definitive evidence that there were people there so that Doc Caldwell and the cop would believe her and help her in coming up with a solution. As it was, the good doctor and the cop had spent most of their time resting and eating and waiting. They felt as safe as they had since that early morning when they had escaped the hospital. But if there was anything that she had learned over the past few days, it was that safety was fleeting and that it was dangerous to get comfortable and complacent. So she watched and waited and hoped for a sign from across the street.

47.

Why does she gotta stand there like that? Does she wanna get us caught? Maybe she's just trying to tease me and the Doc with her ass. Slut. She knows exactly what she's doing. Acting like she can see something across the way. What kind of fool does she take me for?

Why is it that she's the only one who seemed to be able to see signs of actual life in that house? Just wishful thinking. He knew better. He was prepared...his soul was prepared. The End of Days isn't about surviving; it's about judgment and redemption.

It was probably that sense of judgment that had restrained Officer Ivanoff up until then. He had gone back and forth between wanting to strangle her and wanting to take her since they had started their flight. How many days ago was that? He'd lost count. As they settled cozier and cozier into the house though, he was starting to feel that restraint was pointless. And he started to get the sense that she even wanted him to take her. The way that she swayed her hips and shook her hair was full of temptation and she knew it. She was the sort who used her wiles to get her way. He'd come to that conclusion days ago. She was of low moral values and not deserving of respect. She probably didn't want respect. He was starting to think that maybe he should show her a lesson and then maybe she would see the error of her ways.

He looked over at the doctor, who was asleep even then. The doctor turned on the couch and let out a long, slow breath that came from deep down. It was breath full of fear and doubt. The Doc was probably thinking about her too. It was probably going to be up to Mal to get things started. They'll both thank him afterward. He just knew that they would.

The woman could sense some of what he was thinking. At least that was how he interpreted her impression when she looked away from the window back at him. In apparent frustration, she walked away from the window and went down the hall.

Sensing his cue, Officer Ivanoff stood up and very gingerly made his way down the hall after her. Yeah, she was going to appreciate this and so was he. It had been a long time since he had last been with a woman. This time though it would be different. They hadn't been drinking, so there were no doubts and no excuses for anyone.

48.

Seeing his shadow come down the hall after her, Emma shook her head and said, "If you're coming down here to hassle me or to talk about God, then I have to admit that I don't have the energy to deal with you right now."

Standing in the doorway, he didn't say a word to her. He walked through and shut the door behind him, startling her somewhat.

"What do you want Officer?"

"I think you know what I want and it's the same thing that you want so just drop the act. Okay?"

"What the fuck are you talking about?"

"That mouth of yours...You're just trying to get me riled aren't you? Well, honey, I'm already there."

He walked across the room as she retreated toward the closet. "I don't know what you had in mind, but I don't like the way that you're talking to me."

"You know perfectly well what's on my mind." He was leaned forward on the balls of his feet, like a predator ready to pounce. He narrowed his eyes and turned his lips up into a snarl.

"You had just better back the fuck off."

"You say no but I can see that you don't mean it. You're just like all women."

Looking around for anything with which to defend herself, Emma saw nothing. She was in a child's bedroom that was full of safe, soft toys, pillows, and blankets. She backed slowly into the closet and nearly fell over a wooden rocking horse that had been pushed off to the side by its previous rider. He stepped closer as she regained her balance and took her eyes off of him.

Desperate she said, "I said no and I mean no. Now get the fuck away from me."

"Oh sweetie. We're gonna have such fun. You'll see and then you'll regret having made us both wait as long as you did."

Tears full of anger and fear started to spill from her eyes as she continued to back up. The clothes hanging in the closet started to welcome her into their domain like the embracing limbs of a dense forest. She tried to get around him, but he was too close now. He was almost upon her. Her breathing was strained and frightened. His was deep and hungry. He grabbed her by the arm and forced her back farther into the closet. She fell backward, hitting her head on the back wall and sliding down to the floor. He tried to grab her blouse as she fell, but only came away with her nametag that was still on her chest.

Lying there and still desperate for rescue but too terrified to make any loud noises, she looked to both sides and then she laid her eyes on it. Leaning in the corner of the closet was an ancient Louisville Slugger miniature wooden baseball bat. It was the sort of thing that professional baseball teams would give away at season openers and for special events to the first hundred or thousand or however many people to come into the park. It was primarily a toy but it was solid wood and just about the right size for the confined space in which she found herself.

She reached out and grabbed the small bat with her left hand and swung almost in the same motion. The bat found its mark on the police officer's shin. He hopped up onto his other foot almost immediately as the pain registered. She didn't hesitate and swung the bat, trying to hit him in the crotch. She missed and hit him instead on his hip. It was enough though to force him back on his heels. She got to her feet as quickly as possible and came at him, not satisfied with merely defending herself. She wanted to hurt him as much as he wanted to hurt her.

He reached to his hip for his pistol, but remembered that he'd taken off his belt in the living room before following her down the hall. Even his mace was missing. He gritted his teeth and held up his hand to try and calm her. She didn't wait even an instant. She hit him on his upheld hand and then on his arm. He recoiled with the pain but then wheeled around with both of his fists up.

"You fucking bitch. We'll see who's gonna get who. Put that fucking bat down before I really decide to teach you a lesson."

She swung the bat at him, solely with the intention of forcing him back just a little farther so that she could get to the door. He hadn't locked it, so she opened it and backed herself through it, closing it as she did.

He leapt forward and landed hard against the now closed door. He shouted, "You fucking slut!!! You're fucking dead!!"

Already hearing the commotion in his sleep but unable to wake, the shouting was enough to draw Doctor Caldwell to consciousness.

He was just waking and sitting up when Emma came running down the hall with a bat in her hand.

"What is going on?"

"That fucking cop was trying to rape me."

"What?" he asked in disbelief.

Looking down the hallway toward a very angry Officer Ivanoff who was just then coming through the bedroom door, Doctor Caldwell stood up and demanded, "What the hell is going on officer?"

"That bitch invited me back to a bedroom with her and when she changed her mind, she got all defensive and violent. She fucking hit me with a bat."

"I what!?!" but Emma didn't wait for the police officer to repeat his story. She leaned back and let fly the bat. The wooden projectile glanced off of the officer's back as he ducked and then went through the front window. The smashing glass caused both Officer Ivanoff and Doctor Caldwell to cringe, but Emma wasn't done. She looked down and saw the police belt on the reclining chair. She lifted up the holster and made her way around the doctor.

Officer Ivanoff backed away slowly and tried to calm her with, "Now let's not be hasty. The broken window might draw those things' attention but a gunshot definitely will."

"You piece of shit. You act like I should care."

She threw down the belt and holster, having retrieved what

she needed. Malachi Ivanoff ducked his head down behind his hands and lowered himself into a protective crouch. Emma didn't wait for even a moment, she took aim and let loose with the mace she had taken from his belt. The stream of caustic vapor and liquid found its mark, finding the police officer's face, eyes, nose, and mouth. He fully expected to be shot, so when he was only maced, his relief mixed with the wholly unexpected kind of pain that he was experiencing. He fell backward as if he had been shot and screamed.

"My eyes!!! My eyes!!! I can't see!!"

He shouted some more profanities and fell to his knees as he rubbed and rubbed at his stinging burning eyes. "I'll fucking get you, you bitch!"

"Yeah, you already tried once and look where it got you. Go fuck yourself!"

With both of them spent from the past few seconds of activity, there was a sudden quiet that settled over the room. The quiet, of course, was immediately overwhelmed with the sound coming from the street and yard below. The doctor went to the now broken window and looked out.

"Damnit. We gotta get outta here and fast. Can you guys put this behind you until we're clear of this place?"

"Fuck him. Leave him here."

"Don't you dare listen to her Doc. She's the one who caused all of this. I'm a cop for Christ's sake. Who you gonna believe, me or her?"

49.

The shattering glass drew everyone's attention and shored up the opinion that there were people in the house across the street. It had quite obviously also had the same effect on the monsters in the street. It was as if they already suspected that there was fresh meat nearby and had just been waiting for their cue. As a single body, the hundred or so of the things began to congregate outside the house. Milling about in their tattered shreds of clothing and with their grey rotting flesh, the ghouls filled the street. There was an animalistic excitement that swept through the undead bodies. Their tics, random but constant, smoothed considerably with their new focus, though their movement by and large had become much stiffer and rigid. They were rotting and their dexterity was starting to suffer. To Jerry watching from a front window in the bunkered house across the street, this was the best news he'd learned in quite a while. Perhaps they could outlast these things. Maybe they would decompose to a state of immobility. There was hope...perhaps.

He watched and shook his head as the still unrevealed person or people in the house across the street, made a foolish but predictable mistake. From the second floor broken window came hurtling a broken bottle with a flower like flame dancing from its top. The glass hit the pavement in front of the yard and amidst the large group zombies. The resulting flash and fire engulfed close to a dozen of the things, who barely even reacted to the change. The fire went out soon enough, leaving the ghouls smoldering and reeking of burned flesh and hair. Neil had described their smell pretty well from his very close encounter with one of them, but Jerry hadn't been able to smell them himself. The new smell from the impromptu and half-assed attempt at a barbecue in the street was nauseating even through the closed windows of their sanctuary.

And then he chuckled when he saw yet another of the improvised Molotov cocktails tossed out. The second bottle didn't travel nearly as far and exploded with a much larger ball of flame and plume of black smoke. Quite obviously, the second of the bombs was a larger bottle filled with more of whatever flammable liquid had been found. The second blast caught the larger group's attention momentarily. All of the undead eyes seemed to turn themselves at this latest distraction.

50.

"That's it?" asked the doctor.

To which the police officer answered, "Yeah. There's some other things down there that will burn but nothing like what we've already thrown out."

Nodding and biting his lower lip, Doctor Caldwell said soberly, "Well, I guess that's our cue to make our move then."

Feeling the chills on her arms and up her spine again, Emma forced herself to nod and lead the two men down the stairs to the backdoor. Hopefully, none of those things had made their way around to the back of the house yet. They'd find out soon enough though.

Emma and the doctor removed the nails from the pieces of lumber nailed around the doorframe and on the floor in front of the door. When all had been prepared, the doctor looked at Officer Ivanoff and asked him, "You ready."

"Yeah. I guess so."

"Okay. Here we go. One. Two. Thhhhhreeeeeeee!"

The door flew open and out jumped Doctor Caldwell. He hadn't planned on going first, but his adrenaline and all the sugar from the sweets they'd been eating over the past couple of days teamed up against him and substituted impatient bravado for his better judgment. He spun around looking in every direction. So far so good.

He nodded to the other two and gestured with his hand in a manner to signify that all was clear, for the moment. Emma and the police officer quickly followed the doctor out into the backyard and then ran over to the fence.

"What if more of those things are over there in the backyards between here and there and we can't make it," asked the police officer.

More to Emma than to the peace officer, the doctor responded, "By all accounts, we all should probably be dead by now anyway. I guess we just deal with everything as it happens. No point in planning for what we could never predict. You know?"

Remembering that everything starting from the moment that he'd responded to the emergency distress call he'd received to quell a disturbance at Providence Hospital until right then, defied reason and normalcy the police officer just nodded in obvious agreement. The three of them helped one another over the six-foot high cedar fences and got away from their latest refuge, wondering if that would be their last.

Their intention was to traverse all of the backyards that sat between their house and the one that supposedly housed other survivors. It was a gamble, but they all had agreed that getting away from their house was going to be difficult and so far so good.

They were running along the cedar fence in what appeared to be a utility easement. The underbrush was thick and untouched. The going was slow and noisy, their feet crunching the stale and drying growth. Officer Ivanoff, leading the other two, ran with his pistol drawn from its holster. He pushed aside smallish birch tree trunks here and there, sapling firs, and wild raspberry bushes growing everywhere. He didn't look back to verify the other two kept up. It didn't matter to him. It was their job to keep up. He just needed to cut the path and show them the way.

It wasn't like that summer years ago when he moved to Bethel to work with his uncle Simeon. His uncle had his own guiding business. He'd take out groups to hunt moose, fish salmon, or photograph wildlife. They worked from before sunrise most days until almost sunset, keeping in mind that there was only a handful of hours and sometimes less separating the two daily events in the summers on the Lower Kuskokwim River.

He loved the nature of the work. He loved being out on the river or trekking across the land. He knew how to hunt; it was in his blood. He got so excited on his first trip with a group of hunters from Kentucky that he brought down the first bear they encountered. He saw the animal from quite a distance, knelt against a tree, and fired. The gunshot startled everyone in the group, including his uncle. Later that night, Uncle Simeon took him aside and tried to explain that they were not there for themselves. They were there to help these other people who didn't know Alaska to experience what most Alaskans take for granted. It was their job to make sure that the visitors who came to them walked away at the end of the week thinking that they'd just had the trip of a lifetime. And for many of their visitors, it was exactly that.

All summer, Uncle Simeon was correcting him. He walked too fast when they were in thick vegetation. It was hard for the hunters to keep up. He didn't talk enough and explain how and why they did things. He smoked too much and cursed more than he should. He didn't answer questions often and when he did he was too smug. All summer Malachi tried to slow his pace, tried to answer questions, tried to impress his uncle but at summer's end, he was told that he wouldn't be asked to return next year. Uncle Simeon tried to give him a last bit of advice but Malachi wasn't hearing any of it. He wanted his paycheck and his airline ticket to go back to Anchorage and back to civilization where things made more sense to him. He loved to hunt and fish, but he just couldn't hack the village lifestyle.

And now there he was cutting another path though the rough, but this time he didn't have to look back or be concerned that the paying hunters couldn't keep up. If that woman and the doctor couldn't keep pace with him, well that was just their bad luck.

51.

"Is this the house?" Emma asked quietly before they jumped the fence.

Doctor Caldwell looked through the narrow gaps between the slats of treated cedar planks comprising the fence. He looked right and then left through the fence.

"Yeah, I think this is it. I don't see smoke coming from the chimney though."

Emma's eyes widened. "What?"

"Relax. That doesn't necessarily mean anything."

Officer Ivanoff shared under his breath, "This had better not been a wild goose chase."

Emma looked over at him and was all ready to unleash a barrage of obscenity laced accusations but caught Doctor Caldwell's eyes and instead bit her tongue. She instead offered, "Well, getting in there has got to be better than waiting around out here. Right? I mean, we've got to get inside somewhere. Those things will definitely find us out here."

"She's right. Let's get over there and check it out. It looks like the yard is fenced on all four sides, so the likelihood that some of those things are in the backyard is pretty slim. Still, keep your eyes open."

Malachi asked no one in particular, "So, who goes over first?"

Emma said as bluntly as she dared, "Well I guess if you're askin' then we can assume that you don't want to go first and I'm not staying over here with you by myself, so I guess I'll go."

The doctor looked at the police officer and said, "That's ridiculous."

Quickly she responded, "What? That the cop won't actually man up and protect us or that I refuse to be alone with a rapist?"

"You fucking..."

"Stop it goddamnit. Both of you. Regardless of what went on, Emma those comments aren't helping."

Malachi, wounded by the possible suggestion, asked, "What do you mean by 'what went on'?"

"This is neither the time nor the place."

Emma, ending the stalemate, demanded, "Give me a goddamned boost Doc. You keep your fucking hands off."

"Fuck you."

"Doc?"

She crested the fence and stalled to look around from the top. The backyard was empty and the gate was closed securely. She breathed a small sigh of relief for at least this bit of good news. When the backdoor leading from the house to the second story deck opened, she almost wet herself. Standing in the doorway was a chubby blonde woman and young man holding a scoped hunting rifle. Emma looked back down at the two men and said with a smile, "There are people. They're on the deck and waving at me as I speak."

52.

"How many are there?"

Jerry answered immediately, his voice filled with excitement, "I don't know. So far, there is just a woman but I'm guessing there's at least one more."

"Why do you say that?"

"I don't think she got herself over the fence on her own. She just doesn't seem the type."

Neil felt something that he hadn't in some time. He felt hopeful. Maybe this wasn't the end of the world. Maybe this was just a reality check for all of them who had started to take for granted all that they had. Maybe this was just the cold slap in the face that humanity needed to get its shit together.

"What's she doing?" he asked Jerry and Rachel.

"She's in the yard. What is she...? Oh, she's getting the ladder. There must be others there."

"Good. Does she need any help?"

Jerry, while excited about their new and welcome company, continued to look around at the yards and the woods surrounding them. "No, I think she's got it. The ladder is already over the fence. I see two more people coming over. One is a cop."

"Any more?"

"No, that looks like that's about it."

53.

Emma ran over to the deck while Doctor Caldwell and Police Officer Ivanoff were still getting over. The first thing she noticed about the deck was that the bottom half of stairs were gone. They'd been removed and tossed to the ground. The blond woman who had been standing at the door, came over to the edge and offered a hand down to Emma.

"C-mon on up. Quick. Before those things know that you're out here."

The blond woman's jacket, a shiny faux black leather jacket, caught on first a railing edge and then on a long nail, probably used to hang a planter or a bird feeder that was sticking out from the railing. Frustrated, the blond removed her jacket and tossed it up onto a lawn chair that was sitting on the top of the deck.

Hand fully extended, she said, "Here. Take my hand."

Emma gripped the warm, soft hand and, using her other on the lowest wooden step which sat at about eye level, lifted herself up out of the yard. And with all the urgency they could muster, the doctor and the police officer got themselves up as well.

The man, boy really, standing at the doorway and still holding the hunting rifle, suggested, "Let's all get inside. We can introduce ourselves in there."

Emma, tears in her eyes, nodded and smiled, walking past the young man and into the house.

54.

Neil began, "So, do you have any news? Where did you guys come from? How did you get here? Are there others that you know of?"

Doctor Caldwell held up both of his hands to stall the barrage of questions. He shook his head and answered at the same time, "We've been on the run for days now. How long has it been? We haven't heard from or seen anyone since we fled the hospital. We were kind of hoping that maybe you had answers to those same questions. I guess we're all as blind as one another."

Meghan related to them what they had heard on the radio and television before the power and then the signals had died. She told them about a possible defense line established at Knik Arm Bridge but that they didn't know if it had worked or not. She described the chaotic nature of the news reports and how no one seemed to know what was happening. She likened the character of the broadcasts to those of the morning of September 11, 2001 when the World Trade Center had been brought down by a terrorist attack. There was a lot of talking but not a lot being said. There was fear and doubt in the voices from the news reporters and a lot of speculation. And then there was just silence after the power went out. They didn't know what had happened or what was going to happen. She told them about getting away from Midtown Anchorage and finding their way to the house in which they had found refuge. She talked and talked about what they had seen and what they had done. She began to cry when she spoke about hiding in the house and not going out to help those who were being hunted and trapped on the roads outside.

The doctor stopped her and said, "You shouldn't be ashamed. There really probably wasn't anything you or anyone else could have done anyway. We were in the hospital where all of this began...." He stopped suddenly when he realized that he recognized Jerry from the hospital. He couldn't believe his eyes. "Jerry?"

"Yes Doctor Caldwell."

"You made it out?"

"Yeah."

"And those kids?"

"Yeah, they're here too."

That was about the time that Jules and Danny appeared from behind Kim. Doctor Caldwell took a long look at the two children and then smiled at Jerry. "Well done." And that was all that he said, but Jerry could read the rest of what he meant in the Doctor's expression.

Neil asked, "What about you Doctor? How did you make it here?"

The doctor looked at Emma and then at Officer Ivanoff. "Can we sit down and maybe get something to drink?"

For a moment, everyone felt normal again. These three newcomers were treated like guests in a home. They were shown to the dining room table and given some cups with water taken from a large bucket in the sink. They were also given a granola bar and a small package of fruit snacks.

Swallowing a bite of granola that was almost half of the entire snack bar, the doctor began, "We were there, Jerry, the kids, and I, when it all started. There was a child who was brought to the hospital by his parents. He'd been bitten by something. It was assumed that it was some kind of wild animal but these two kids insisted that it was a...a caveman; I believe is what they called it. Regardless, the boy worsened by the second and then he just died. We tried to revive him but there was nothing we could do for him. His little body was just too weak...too fragile."

He looked over at the two children who were still standing in the living room, just steps away from him, and apologized, "We tried and tried, but we just couldn't do anything for him. Your brother died."

A bit confused but wanting to know, Jules asked in her timid little voice, "What about Mommy and Daddy?"

The doctor shook his head and his eyes watery and sad, he said, "No. I don't think they made it either." To the others he continued, "That's where it all started, like I said. Everything happened so quickly and so tragically. As one was getting knocked down, another was getting up. Things got out of control all at once. There was nothing anyone could do to stop any of it. It all just happened so quickly."

He told them of their retreat through the hospital and how their group was steadily whittled away. He told them about Simon and how he had helped them only to fall victim to the fiends himself. When he spoke about the helicopter and their escape from the hospital, he heard his two companions finally exhale. They'd been holding their breaths while he spoke. They were reliving their flight and their fear in their own minds as he spoke. They couldn't help it. While it was happening, it had all gone by in such a blur of violence and death. This had been the first time that any of them had talked about it...the first time that any of them had reflected on it out loud.

"And so now here we are."

Tony said somberly, "Amen."

Doctor Caldwell looked up at him and nodded. "Amen indeed."

55.

It was a handful of hours later. The newcomers, Emma and Doctor Caldwell anyway, changed into new clothes. Emma had forgotten what it was like to wear comfortable shoes as she slipped on the sneakers taken from a woman's closet. It was necessary for all of them to wear shoes and sweatshirts and whatever else they could find to stay warm. Despite the fire still burning in the fireplace, it was getting cooler and cooler in the house. There was no denying it. And their woodpile was getting smaller and smaller. They couldn't continue to burn wood indefinitely.

Rachel walked from room to room looking for something. Finally, Jules, after having watched her frantically searching, asked her, "Whatcha lookin' for?"

"My coat. I'm looking for my coat. You remember what it looked like?"

"Yeah, it was a cool, shiny black one. It was pretty."

Rachel smiled and touched the child's head, "Yeah, it is a cool jacket isn't it? My Mom gave that to me for my birthday."

"Your birthday? When did you have that?"

"About two weeks ago."

"Did you go to Chuck E. Cheese?"

Smiling and laughing a little, Rachel answered, "No, I guess I missed out, huh."

"Yeah, they got the best pizza and have you ever played skeet ball?"

"Yeah, I think I have."

"That's the best and then you get tickets and you can go get cool stuff at the shop. Last time we went, I didn't have enough tickets to get the purse and make-up that I wanted so Marty gave me some of his tickets. Danny did too. I still have the purse but I used up all the make-up."

"Did you have fun?"

"Uh-huh. But it wasn't my birthday then. We just went because we'd all been good and Mom said that if we were good and quiet on Saturday then we could go on Sunday as a treat."

"I guess you were good then."

"Yeah. If you didn't go to Chuck E. Cheese, then where did you go?"

"My Mom took me out to dinner at a place called Glacier Brewhouse. We had a really nice dinner and we talked and talked. It's nice just to sit and talk with your Mom sometimes." Feeling herself start to get emotional, Rachel turned away and said, "Well, my Mom gave me the jacket that night. She knew that I wanted it but knew that I'd never buy it for myself. She just wanted me to have it."

"I'll help you find it."

"Thanks kid...Jules, I mean."

"You're welcome. My Mom always asks me 'Where do you remember seeing it last?'"

Crying now, Rachel said, "Mine too Jules. Mine too."

They looked upstairs and down but could not locate it. They even looked out in the garage, despite the fact that Rachel couldn't remember the last time that she'd even been in that room. Someone may have moved it on her and set it in there by mistake. They looked and looked but in the end their search came up empty.

It was early afternoon by then and things had started to settle down. Most of the activity in the house was happening, not surprisingly, around the fire. There wasn't anything specific that was happening really. They were just hanging out and waiting, activities that had become the mainstay of their day-to-day lives.

Emma wasn't in the room. She was down the hall in one of the bedrooms. She was still angry and hurt by what had happened between her and Officer Ivanoff. She couldn't be in the same room with him anymore. She was frankly concerned that she wouldn't be able to control herself around him anymore and fly off in a rage that might just leave him dead. She was carrying one of the pistols that Neil had scavenged from Fred Meyer. It was a smallish silver revolver that smelled of oil and was somewhat heavy in her hand. Deep down, she hoped that he'd try it again and she could stop him permanently. As it was, she just avoided being around him. She figured that was just the safest thing for all of them because she knew that a gunshot would certainly give their sanctuary away. She wouldn't, however, hesitate to use the gun, regardless of consequences, if he ever came at her like that again.

For his part, Officer Malachi was downstairs alone in the darkness of the boarded up family room. He sat down there staring at the blank television screen. He was remembering past football games that he'd watched on his own television. He missed his ritual. Living in Alaska, he'd grown accustomed to the fact that NFL games started early in the morning. The hassle of having to wake early on Sunday mornings to catch the games, especially Seattle Seahawks games, wore off after a very short time.

Sitting down in the dimly lit basement family room, he was suddenly startled to see his youthful cousin sitting comfortably with his feet up on the couch. His boyish frame and smiling face appeared exceptionally comfortable on the small couch. His father too was there, standing in the doorway with a bag of his favorite chips, Lays Barbecue. The Seahawks had the ball and were all set to snap. The three of them held their breath while they watched Hasselbeck scramble behind his defensive line. He didn't seem to be able to find a target and then he saw him; a streaking receiver running along the sideline. He arched back and tossed the ball, a perfect spiral, into the air.

Malachi could feel his heart begin to race. Would he catch that pass? It seemed like such a long shot. If he did though, it was smooth sailing all the way to the end zone. He looked over at his cousin. He was chewing feverishly on his snack of choice, Slim Jim beef sticks. He returned Malachi's stare and smiled.

When he looked back, the television wasn't on anymore. He was back in the dark room. His father was gone as was his cousin. He was alone again. He stood up from the recliner and moved to the small couch. He touched where his cousin had been sitting and felt around for any evidence that he or anyone had been there. The fabric was cold and the empty wrappers from the beef sticks weren't there anymore either. He massaged his sweaty forehead and temples, trying to will away the doubt and confusion. They had been here with him but how? And where were they now?

He sat down on the couch and about screamed when he looked over and saw his father sitting in the Lazyboy recliner. "What's wrong Mal?"

"Daddy?"

"Yeah buddy. I'm here. What's wrong?"

"I...I...but how...where...aren't you...?"

"Just like you Mal. Can't put together a single thought and get it out of your mouth. Nothing's changed has it?"

With his eyes as wide as his mouth, Malachi looked around. The game was gone from the television and his cousin was still absent, but his father was definitely there.

"How long have you been here, daddy?"

"What do you mean by that, little man?"

"You know I don't like it when you call me that."

"Father's right I guess."

"Why are you here?"

His father, still watching the blank television screen, asked, "Why are you?"

"What do you mean? We had to come here or else we would have been..."

"Would have been what? Have you been a bad boy again?"

"No daddy. I just...we just..."

"You and your friends haven't been setting fires again have you?"

"No daddy. I've been a good boy."

"You'd better. Remember what happened to your cousin at the school?"

"Yes daddy. I remember. I haven't been playing with matches. I learned my lesson. You don't have to..."

There was a long pause in which Malachi looked around the room again. When he looked back at the recliner, his father was gone. Malachi's childhood uncertainty, long forgotten and set aside, was still there though. The soreness of bruises from decades ago returned to his arms and shoulders; he could almost feel the

228

knuckle indentations on his skin.

He heard a voice again but couldn't make it out clearly. He heard it again. He looked around trying to figure out from where it was coming. He couldn't make out the words let alone their source. He held his breath and concentrated.

"Officer? Officer? Are you hungry?"

He opened his clinched eyes and saw a big Asian guy standing in the doorway now. It took a second more before he recognized the man as Tony from upstairs. He looked at the man for a good long while. He bit his lower lip, chewing on the raw, chapped skin there.

Tony waited a moment longer and then entered the seemingly subterranean room. It felt like a dungeon down there. The meager light coming in around the edges of the plywood covering the outside of the window barely provided any illumination at all. He was afraid that he might be disturbing or even waking the man. Though he couldn't see him well, Tony could sense a degree of uncertainty in the other man's body language. He stalled a second or two longer, hoping that the other man would speak up or at least acknowledge his presence in the room.

"Are you okay?"

Officer Ivanoff finally leaned back and said, "I'm good."

"You hungry?"

"Naw, I'm good. If I get hungry, I'll come up."

"D'you want some company down here?"

Shaking his head, "Naw, I'm good."

"Okay. You need anything, just holler."

At that, Tony went back upstairs. He found Doctor Caldwell sitting in the kitchen with Emma, Neil, and Meghan. Tony leaned into the wall and waited for the discussion to come to a pause, at which point he could interrupt. They were talking about what they had seen and where. The doctor was describing the numerous police barricades they'd seen while they overflew them in the helicopter. Neil had an Anchorage city street map on the table between all of them and was moving it around to mark the locations of each of these failed barricades. They were trying to plot probable escape routes and identifying alternate routes around possible roadblocks and problem spots.

Finally, Tony couldn't wait anymore. He looked over his

shoulder to make sure that he was only talking with the four people at the table. "Guys, I don't know if that cop downstairs is doing alright."

Emma spread a knowing smile across her face and said acidly, "That guy only wears a cop uniform. He's nowhere near being an actual cop. No cops I've ever known would or even could do the things that he's done."

Doctor Caldwell understood Emma's comment but everyone else's faces were questioning. Emma was about to clarify for all of them when she caught the doctor's eyes and thought better of it. She accepted the fact that there would be a more appropriate place for Malachi to have to answer for what he tried to do to her and then for his cowardly behavior. She didn't like it, but she did trust Doctor Caldwell's judgment.

The doctor looked at Tony and asked for him to elaborate.

"Well, I was down there with him for a few seconds but I don't think he knew that I was there. He was looking right at me but he just didn't know. And then, when he did realize that someone was in the room with him, I don't think that he knew that it was me. I mean, I've seen some blank stares in my time and even some nasty glares, but he was totally...absent."

Caldwell asked, "What was he doing?"

"Nothing. Just sitting there watching a blank tv screen."

"Did he threaten you or appear to be a danger to himself?"

"No. He just didn't seem right to me."

"It's probably just exhaustion. Give him some room and if he wants to stay down there by himself, well, we'll just have to accommodate him on that one. Let's all keep an eye on him though."

Emma added, "Yeah, we don't need a Columbine or Virginia Tech on our hands."

With that comment, Neil was suddenly concerned with the presence of the newcomers. He could tell that there was something more going on, especially with Emma, but he wasn't sure what it was. He needed to know because they couldn't afford any surprises. There just wasn't any room for problems in their little sanctuary.

Forgetting about his unease when he was downstairs, Tony began to munch on a can of Hormel chili that had been cooked in the fire. He asked, "So what's going on?"

Neil started to explain that they were just trying to prepare for contingencies, when he was interrupted by a quiet, but clearly audible electronic tone that repeated and repeated and repeated. It was a cell phone. It was Rachel's cell phone. She realized it almost immediately. Her phone was in her jacket and her jacket was...outside.

She'd taken it off to help Emma, the police officer, and the doctor while they were trying to climb up onto the deck. It was still sitting out back on the side railing of the deck. It was outside ringing and ringing.

Rachel, who was sitting in the living room hanging out with Jules, leapt to her feet and ran to the back door. She saw her jacket and flew outside to retrieve it. She fumbled with the pockets until she found the phone and powered it off.

Neil looked at her with both hope and terror in his eyes. She shook her head and said apologetically, "It was just my alarm. It's time for my annual doctor's appointment. I turned the phone on earlier to see if we'd gotten a cell signal yet and I guess I forgot to turn it off. Sorry."

Jerry, who had positioned himself at the front window, said, "Guys. They know that we're here now. Come take a peek."

Outside in the street, the crowd of zombies, who had been just gathering and waiting, all began to turn and walk over to the house. Their movements, which had become up to that point slow and stiff, became more organic. Their steps picked up pace as the excitement grew in the crowd. They had been detecting odors of the living for some time, but hadn't been able to pinpoint the source. The noise was all that it took.

There were probably more than a hundred of them in the street by then. They gathered around the front of the house and began to pound the siding with their fists, their feet, and even their heads. A few made their way up the short flight of steps leading up to the porch and started to bang on the front door.

Neil's fear suddenly gripped him again. They didn't have much of a choice any longer. They were going to have to go outside and face these things. Their refuge had been found out and it was just a matter of time before it would be breached. He felt that familiar chill on his arms, his legs, and up his spine. He also felt a sense of despair start to nag at him. He had begun to believe that they might all make it out alive, but that feeling all at once faded. He knew that they were in trouble.

Rachel could tell that she had just let the air out of everyone's balloon. She was crying and begging for forgiveness. Kim left the front window, having seen enough already, and went over to Rachel who was sitting on the floor. Rachel's long permed blonde hair was covering her face as she slumped forward. Her tears, obscured by the blonde curtain, coursed down her splotchy red cheeks and dampened her too-tight scavenged sweater. Kim tried to console her by rubbing her hunched shoulders and speaking kind words, but she knew if was all for naught. Under her breath Rachel sobbed to herself, "I've doomed us all." Kim wanted to tell her that it was just an accident and that all hope wasn't lost, but she couldn't bring herself to do it. Those words may have been the right things to say, but the words simply wouldn't come.

Kim wanted to tell her that she was wrong. She really wanted to believe that Rachel was wrong, but the persistent silence that had reigned the streets for so many days refused to hear any of it. Kim's doubt quieted her comfort to both Rachel and herself. She was understandably concerned that Rachel was painfully correct in her assessment. Of course Kim didn't want to believe that, but Rachel's words flashed bright and undeniable.

The pounding on the walls and doors was bad enough but it didn't appear to be all that they could expect. With the ghouls closer, a cloud of rot-filled air seemed to settle over the house, finding its way in through any seam or opening that presented itself. It was an odor that clung to clothing, carpet, and hair. There was no suppressing it with candles or air freshener–Kim tried. Jerry threw more wood onto the fire hoping that the warm air rising up the chimney would prevent some of the foul stench from trickling down. Nothing they did seemed to make any difference at all. After trying to deal with it for quite some time and nothing working, they all seemed to accept the fact that the reek was there to stay and the only way to get away from it was to get away from the house. Neil remembered a segment from a history book in a college class from years ago. It was an entry about the American Civil War and, more specifically, the aftermath of the Battle of Gettysburg...or was it Antietam. He couldn't remember for sure.

What he did recall about the passage was the description of the battlefield. It was so vivid to him. The writer described a scene with bodies, several days after the battle's end, still strewn across farm fields, on roads and footpaths, near streams and amidst trees. The writer wrote about the pungence that seemed to permeate the very air being breathed...of the sense that the air itself was poison. He thought about that passage as he struggled to breathe shallowly, trying not to inhale any more of the reeking foulness than he absolutely must in order to survive. He felt himself stifle the urge from his churning, revolting stomach to vomit several times early on during that day.

Dr. Caldwell offered a temporary and less than ideal solution. He took a bandana from a drawer in a child's bedroom, soaked it with perfume, and then tied it over his mouth and nose. It wasn't perfect, but it made it so that he could keep working without having to fight the rising nausea every few moments. The others followed his lead; using any cloth they could find to become a makeshift surgical mask. To observe them was like watching a ragtag and under-equipped aid group dealing with a plague in a third world nation. They were all sweaty and filthy and their masks were rapidly becoming dingy.

Jerry, Meghan, Kim, and Dr. Caldwell were all rolling blankets into tight bundles in preparation for making a run for a new refuge. Neil and Tony were downstairs in the garage loading supplies into and onto the van. The stark reality of their situation was clearly evident to all of them though. They only had a minvan, which typically could seat seven safely, in which to transport nine adults and two children. Neil thought they could pile supplies onto the top of the minivan, despite the fact that there wasn't a cargo rack on the vehicle. He felt that they could position items on the top and then tie them down so that they could mutually support staying in place. He didn't know if it would work or not, but he was willing to try and Tony was more than willing to help.

Of course, while they worked, a legion of undead pounded themselves against the closed garage doors. Their persistent and mind-numbing moaning was all the more loud in the garage than it was in the much more insulated house. The constant sound solicited a nausea that was not unlike motion sickness.

"Could it get any worse?" asked Tony to no one in particular.

Neil looked at him sardonically and said, "One thing I've learned lately is to not ask that question because..."

"Yeah, I know. Sorry."

"Let's just get this all taken care of and then figure out what our next step is."

"You got it boss. Do you really think that we can get away from here?"

Neil had his doubts; they all did. He had to believe that it was possible though. If he couldn't believe that, then why was he down in the garage loading up the van.

Back upstairs; all of them were in the living room trying to decide the answers to Neil's questions. Officer Ivanoff had joined them again, though he sat on the floor at the top of the stairs away from the larger group. He was sharing the same room with the others, but the distance separating him from the others was still all but insurmountable.

Rachel asked, "Why don't we just sit in here and shoot all of them down from safety."

Kim joined in, "Yeah, maybe if we kill enough of them then the others will get the point that we're not on the menu. I mean... any reasonable..."

Jerry jumped on that comment. "Reasonable? Don't kid yourself. Don't any of you make that mistake. They...these things don't have the faculties for reason anymore. Come'ere."

He led Kim to the window and directed her eyes. "There. That one. Look at it. Do you see it? The one that used to be a bald guy? Looks like he might be wearing a butcher's apron... how fitting. Do you see the one I'm talking about?"

"Yeah."

"Look at his eyes. I mean really look at them. Do you see any inkling of reason left there? Look. Try to see any semblance of humanity." To everyone else he continued, "These aren't people anymore. They're just barely animals. At least you can scare an animal off if you do the right things. These things don't scare. They don't reason...weigh their options. More importantly, they won't hesitate and they won't show you any pity. If you see one of those things that looks like someone you might have known, don't expect it to show you any mercy. I'm only saying that to remind everyone how bad it can get if we're not all on the same sheet of music. We've been relatively safe and very lucky so far. Don't let that get any of us complacent."

Answering Rachel's original question, Neil said, "We don't have enough bullets to shoot all of those things anyway and with each shot, we'll probably attract more of them."

Meghan asked him, "What are you thinking Neil?"

Remembering that hesitation kills, Neil jumped right into the obvious, "We can get all of us in the car and haul ass outta here. Getting started is going to be the hardest part of it. Once we get going though, if we don't slow down at all, I think we can get away from the crowds. The only question is which direction? I think it's safe to assume that both highways outta town will be jammed with stalled vehicles, so the car is only going to get us so far."

Tony suggested, "Why don't we just get away from these things here and find ourselves another hiding spot somewhere else?"

Dr. Caldwell asked, "And then what?"

"What do you mean?"

"I mean, after we find another hiding spot, how long do we stay there? We only have so much food and water. We can't wait indefinitely."

Kim asked, "What if we find another supply stash somewhere? Another store with some more food. Maybe we can find enough to...ah, never mind."

Neil rubbed his chin and thought. That wasn't a half bad idea. They could just get away from this crowd, avoid being seen by others, and then find a spot to hide away for a bit. If they chose the right spot in the right part of town, they could get close enough to a Fred Meyer or Carr's to go scavenging for supplies. They could see if there was a way to wait this all out. Maybe there was still a way.

That was a big list of maybes. Perhaps the biggest list of maybes since Thomas Jefferson last walked through one of his busy cotton fields. Perhaps even a bigger list of maybes than when Neil went shopping for condoms for the first time before what was to be a very promising weekend–it wasn't. With maybes though, there are options and with options there was the scant possibility of hope. Those thoughts ran through his head as a smile, the first in several days, spread, slowly and tentatively, across his face.

"Kim, that's not a half bad idea. Let's talk about that for a bit. We can take it a little bit at a time. No need to be in a rush. Let's figure it all out, and, believe me, there's going to be a lot to figure out before we hightail it outta here. I think the first thing we should get settled is where. Where do we head?"

56.

They talked and talked. Everyone more or less agreed that they should start heading north. There were more avenues of escape heading north...more options. Neil was really starting to appreciate options.

While they discussed it, Neil, Jerry, and Doctor Caldwell started piling firewood from the garage against the front door to try and shore it up a little. The physics of the porch out front made it all but impossible to have more than a couple of those things exerting pressure against the door, but they all decided that it was better to be safe than sorry. The added weight from the piled firewood helped to add a little security.

More of the ghouls had come to help with the siege and more were still on the way. There were still a few in the street, but the vast majority of them were pressed against the front three walls of the house, pounding against them with their firsts, their heads, and their bodies. With all the pressure, Neil and the others were starting to get worried about the window downstairs. They'd covered it over with a large sheet of plywood and then covered the inside with a tarp, but it just didn't seem enough to any of them anymore.

And it wasn't. On the second day of packing and planning, the window, which was behind the plywood, shattered. It was still in its frame, but the glass was as webbed as an arachnid's home. With no other options to cover the potential weak spot, Neil and Doctor Caldwell elected to remove a bedroom door from its hinges and hang it across the inside of the window.

The doctor said as they worked, "You know that if they get through the plywood outside that this door isn't going to hold them at bay for very long don't you?"

"Hopefully we won't be here long enough to test that limit."

"Yeah...hopefully."

Sitting in the same room while they worked but never getting up from his roost on the small couch, Officer Ivanoff didn't participate in the conversation and seldom took his eyes from the blank television screen. He would alternate between reclining back on the worn cushions of the seat and leaning forward with both of his hands on his knees. Several times, Neil and Doc Caldwell looked at one another when the man changed his position. The police officer was a problem all his own. Neil had heard the story about what happened between Emma and him. Doctor Caldwell had related it as candidly and dispassionately as he was able.

Neil wasn't quite sure what to think or how to treat the situation. Officer Ivanoff wasn't making it easy either. His behavior had all of them on edge. In fact, most of the people in the house, including those who weren't privy to the details of the goings on in the other house, just kept their distance from him. Neil knew that they weren't going to be able to avoid Malachi for long, but for the time being it seemed to be the best thing to do. If Malachi was having a psychotic episode though, the pistol on his hip made both Dr. Caldwell and Neil very nervous.

57.

"I think we're ready."

Neil looked at Emma and then at Meghan, who had just spoken. He, of course, had been dreading this moment. Secretly, deep down he guessed he'd been hoping that things would have changed before then so that they wouldn't have to go outside and confront the horrors that awaited them. He could only hope that he would rise up to the challenge. He knew that if he did, it would happen without his thinking about it. If he had to think about it, then there was little to no chance that he would be able to act. Just imagining going outside had kept sleep at bay a number of times since he and Tony had ventured down the street. Even Meghan sleeping next to him hadn't allayed his fears much. While they worked, it was easy for him to stay occupied and avoid thinking about the possibility, but as the work was slowly wrapped up it became increasingly difficult to find distractions. And now, with Meghan's statement there would be no more denying the reality of their situation. They were soon going to be on their way.

Tony asked, "Has anyone thought about how we are going to get out?"

All eyes turned to Dr. Caldwell and Neil. Neither of them had even begun to think about that. They'd been busy plotting a route away from their sanctuary, trying to avoid the main streets and the most likely spots of high vehicle congestion. They'd considered what of the dwindling supplies to load into the vehicle and where to sit people to maximize their limited space. They'd thought about all of that, but hadn't given much thought to their very first step.

Kim suggested again, "Maybe we could just shoot a bunch of them and make it so that we can get out while they regroup."

Neil, doubting the effect of that ploy, said nonetheless, "Yeah, maybe."

Kim, like a dejected child said, "Well, it was just an idea."

Sensing her disappointment, Neil followed up with, "Kim, it isn't a horrible idea. I just don't know if it will work. Have you ever seen any war movies about like the Revolution or the Civil War or anything?"

"I guess so. Why?"

"Well, I'm afraid that what will likely happen, just like with those lines of soldiers from those movies, that as one of the things is shot down from the front rank another of them will move forward and fill his space. There may be no way to shoot enough of them fast enough to make an opening."

"Okay. I see your point."

Dr. Caldwell interjected, "What we need is a distraction."

From the window, Tony said in a matter of fact manner, "I've done my part with distractions. No more going out there to start another fire."

Emma suggested, "Maybe we could just forget about the car and make our way out on foot. Go out the back and sneak away."

Rachel said dryly, "And how far do you think we'll get before they smell us out? And then where will we be, huh? On foot and out in the open? My fat ass, sorry kids, can't move that quick and what about the kids. How long can they keep up?"

Emma shot back, "Well, what's your idea? We've gotta be able to open the garage door and get out. We can't do that with those things standing out there, unless you're planning on opening the door for the rest of us."

"Not likely."

"That's what I thought. If we can't get the door open, then we've gotta think of other options. Right?"

Danny, sitting on the fringes of the group and watching Neil, got an idea. He got up and ran downstairs to the bookcase in the hallway. He remembered seeing some keys there and thought that they might be Meghan's. He found the keys on the top of the low bookcase and, peeking in at Officer Ivanoff as he darted by, ran upstairs with the keys jingling and jangling as he went.

Neil asked, "Whatcha got there Danny?"

"Keys."

Meghan, recognizing the Hawaii key chain her fiancée had gotten for her from a trip down to the island paradise a number of years back, said, "Those are mine."

"Yeah. Does this alarm thingy work?"

"Well, yeah. Why? You afraid someone is going to try and steal my car?"

"No but..."

Neil saw where Danny was headed and finished his thought for him, "But you can set off the alarm with your Panic Button can't you?"

"Yeah," and Meghan realized the possibility too.

Neil began, "Well, we can hit that button and see if it draws those things away. Then we can get that door open and get the hell outta Dodge."

Neil looked over at Danny and gave him a thumbs up sign. "Good job Danny. You may have just come up with the opening that we needed."

Danny smiled and felt more a part of the group finally. He'd contributed and maybe saved all of their lives. And more importantly, he'd impressed Neil. Regardless of the situation, Danny felt like Neil and Jerry were the two coolest adults he'd ever met. They were smart and nice and listened to what he had to say. And the cool thing about that, to him, was that he wasn't a son, a nephew, or any other relation to these guys other than just a kid that got hooked up with them under some pretty bad circumstances. They didn't have to show him any attention or any respect and yet both did. He was glad that, if he had to be trapped with anyone, at least he was spending his time with these two guys. The others weren't bad either, although that cop really kind of freaked him out a little. When he went downstairs to get Meghan's keys, that cop was just sitting there. It looked like he was watching TV, but that couldn't be possible. Danny wasn't even quite sure that the cop noticed him when he looked in at him, even though he'd stood in the doorway plain as day.

That guy just gave him the creeps. The others were all right, he guessed. They weren't mean to him or to Jules, but they treated both of them the way most adults treated them. He'd heard the phrase, "Children should be seen and not heard," before and he felt like most of the people in the house lived by that standard. At least they had since he'd been around them. Neil and Jerry though were different. They were good guys and he knew that he could trust them to look out for him and Jules. In movies and in games, for the most part, kids didn't die and he thought that if anyone could help that to become a reality it was Neil and Jerry.

Neil took the keys from Danny and gave them to Meghan. "Will the alarm still work with the car problems you've been having?"

"Yeah, the alarm was never the problem. It was always the engine...the fuel pump to be exact. What are you thinking then?"

58.

It was decided that Tony would open the garage door. He was the strongest and most fit person in the group and, therefore, stood the best chance of getting the door up quickly and getting himself into the van. Kim wasn't too thrilled with the idea, but even she conceded that he was the most likely choice. Dr. Caldwell offered to help in getting the door up, but having to get a second person into the car and then get moving quickly just didn't seem to make much sense to any of them.

Everyone except Neil, Dr. Caldwell, and Tony loaded themselves into the vehicle. It took both Jerry and Neil to coax Officer Ivanoff out of his room downstairs and into the van. When they entered the television room, he looked at them with confusion in his eyes at first. Neil was convinced that the man either wasn't hearing or didn't understand him when he first began to speak. Finally, after explaining the plan and need to get going right away, the police officer stood up and walked out to the garage. When he saw all the people in the van, he turned around and started to walk back inside. He didn't say a word to anyone.

Jerry, who was coming back downstairs after a final walk through of the living room and the upstairs bedrooms, caught sight of him going back into the downstairs room again. "Officer. Officer. Hey Mal. Where're you goin?"

"I don't think I'm supposed to be here."

"That's why we're leaving. None of us are supposed to be here. This is all just a mistake of colossal proportions. We need to get going right away though. Do you think you can get yourself

243

into the van so we can get to it?"

"The van?"

"Yeah. The one out in the garage. We need you to sit on the middle bench seat and be ready to close the door after Tony gets in from opening the garage door."

"Tony?"

"Yeah. You know. Tony. The big guy."

"He's going to hell you know."

"What?"

"Sodomites. They're all going to hell."

"Well, I don't know anything about that."

"I do. They're all to be damned."

"Mal, can we worry about that later. Right now, Tony is going to help all of us get out of here and for that I think that we all can cut him a little bit of a break. Don't you?"

The police officer shuffled back out toward the garage mumbling unintelligibly for the most part. He sat himself down in his assigned seat and didn't say a word to or look at anyone around him. Jerry climbed into the small space set aside for him in the back seat next to Emma and Kim who each had a child in her lap. Rachel was supposed to be sitting on the bench between Meghan and Officer Malachi, but was, at present, standing/ stooping partially between the two front seats. She just appeared to be anxious and worried and unable to sit.

Neil, Dr. Caldwell, and Tony were all standing in the upstairs window looking down at the yard and street below them. It was amazing to think and remember that those things that were even then hungering for their flesh were once ordinary human beings. The vibrations in the air from their constant moaning had continued to rise in amplitude.

Tony said to the others, "It's a good thing that we're leaving. I don't know how much longer I can take the sound."

Dr. Caldwell added, "Or the smell. And I'm a doctor. But the aroma of rotten flesh is downright overpowering for even me. I can only imagine what it's like for everyone else."

Neil jumped in, "Hopefully we won't have to deal with much more of either. If we can get ahead of those things and just keep them behind us, we might just be okay. It's not the sound or the smell that bothers me the most. It's their teeth that worry me.

We ready?"

The other two nodded and stepped away from the window. Neil lingered just a second longer. He hoped they were making the right decision. He was afraid that there would be no recovering from it if this was a mistake. And if it were a mistake, the error would be fatal for all of them. He swallowed hard and closed his eyes. He wasn't much for praying. He wasn't even much for believing in that sort of thing, but he found himself wondering more at that moment than he had in decades. And then he wondered about those ghouls outside. If there was a higher power of some sort, had their souls ascended or were they trapped? Trapped? He remembered a scene from the movie <u>The Exorcist</u> in which the little possessed girl's mother showed the attending priest her daughter's stomach. At first there was nothing, but slowly, and with the appropriate accompanying music, the words "help me" appeared on her skin from the inside out. That scene had always tugged at the terror strings in his own belly. She was still in there and the demon was tormenting her. She was still in there but had no control whatsoever of her body or her faculties. She was still in there. He wondered for just a heartbeat if those poor souls out on the front lawn were still in their battered and decomposing bodies. Was it a form of purgatory or damnation? He couldn't even begin to imagine and hoped that he would never have to find out for himself.

Realizing he was alone now, he took one last look around. The fire was still burning in the fireplace warming a room that was carpeted with colorful pillows and blankets scattered all over the floor and furniture. The kitchen table had empty cracker boxes and opened plastic wrappers on and under it. There was a disorderliness to it that resembled a more comfortable than typical refugee camp. It was time to move and he knew it.

He removed Meghan's keys from his pocket and looked out again. The zombies were crushing themselves against the house with more and more desperation. They bit and clawed and pounded their fists against the walls, doors, and boarded up window. Neil said aloud to the empty room, "Christ I hope this works." He pressed his thumb against the remote's panic button and from down the street came the echoing clarion cry of Meghan's car's alarm.

He looked down again at the beasts outside. There was a pause for all of them, including Neil, while everyone tried to figure out what that sound was. The walking corpses leaned away from the house at first, not moving but stopping their persistent assault on its walls. Starting with those furthest away from the walls, the things started to turn away in the direction of the new sound. Was that the sound of food? With some anxiousness to their steps, as a group they began to shuffle toward the possibility.

Neil realized that the remote was also for an Autostart installed on the car. Maybe a little more incentive would draw them away quicker. He hit the buttons to start the car and hoped that it had had the desired effect. He didn't know for sure, but it seemed the things in the street picked up their pace, so he thought that maybe it had worked. And it was working. They were leaving the house and giving them an opportunity.

He didn't hesitate for even a moment longer. He flew down the stairs, only alighting on perhaps two steps per flight and was in the garage almost immediately.

Tony was standing near the garage door and taking in short, shallow breaths like a swimmer getting ready to start a race.

"Did it work?" he asked.

Neil nodded his head and said, "Yeah, I think so. They cleared out as soon as the alarm went off. I think we're good...for now."

Neil hopped into the automobile and turned the ignition. The engine in the minivan came to life and everyone in the vehicle breathed an audible sigh of relief. Tony smiled at Kim, who was sitting in the backseat, reached down to grab the bottom of the heavy, insulated garage door, and lifted it open.

59.

Kim was still watching as the three ghouls still standing on the outside of the garage door leapt into the garage and grabbed hold of Tony. He still had his hands on the garage door handles now well above his head. He was all but defenseless as their hands locked onto his reaching arms. Kim screamed. Tony did too when the first one bit him on the soft underside of his right arm. The thing pulled away with a mouthful of dripping red flesh. Not pausing to even chew, it went back for another bite; this time on Tony's shoulder.

Tony was trying to fight them off, but they were all over him all at once. Rachel, still standing in the minivan, leaned down and grabbed the shotgun between the two front seats. She leaned out of the still open side door and fired. The blast knocked her down and out of the minivan and caught Tony's closest attacker across his back and neck. The shot also hit Tony on the right side of his chest, peppering his white shirt with a pattern of red. He and the three attackers all fell back against the garage door.

Rachel, now lying on the garage floor, stood up and screamed. She didn't wait for even a second and ran, still screaming into the house. Jerry, sitting in the back seat, leaned forward quickly and slammed the side door shut.

Kim shouted, "What the fuck are you doing?"

"I don't want those things in here. Do you?"

"But what about Tony...and Rachel?"

The three ghouls, thankfully, ran past the minivan and its passengers and elected to follow Rachel into the house. Dr.

Caldwell looked over at Neil with a question in his eye. There wasn't a whole lot of time so a decision had to be made. Rachel screamed again from inside. This time, there was pain mixed with terror.

From behind him, Neil heard Meghan say, "Just go. Get us outta here Neil."

Kim about came unglued. "What!!!???"

"There's nothing that can be done."

"But Tony...and Rachel. We can't just..."

Meghan ignored Kim's objection. "Just go Neil."

"You cold, goddamned bitch! What kind of a person are you anyway?"

Emma though said, "She's right Neil. Go. They're gone and we're not, so long as we don't sit here."

Neil shifted the vehicle into reverse and hit the gas. They lurched out of the garage, hitting another of the zombies who was coming up the driveway. Neil looked over at Tony who was lying motionless on a pile of topsoil bags stacked in the near corner of the garage. Rachel was still screaming from in the house. Dr. Caldwell looked at Neil again and nodded.

Kim was still protesting from the back. She was still looking into the garage after they were out and were reversing deeper into the cul de sac. Emma asked, "Where are you going Neil? There's nowhere to go this direction."

Neil didn't pause to answer. He just kept reversing until he had pulled the van into a driveway. He then shifted into drive and shot the vehicle forward. He tossed Meghan's keys to Dr. Caldwell and said, "Doc, hit the panic button at the right time."

"The right time?"

"Yeah. I think you'll know when."

Kim saw some movement in the garage and screamed with excitement. "It's Tony! He's alive! We gotta pick him up!"

When Neil didn't stop, she shouted, "Stop the fucking car! Tony's alive! He needs our help!"

But Tony wasn't alive anymore and it became readily apparent as his face came into focus for everyone in the car. The rage and fury in his eyes was vacant and pure. He had become one of them and it had only taken a few moments. Kim was wailing and blubbering in the back seat. She couldn't and therefore refused to see Tony as anything other than what he once was. In her mind and in her heart, Tony was still the same. He just needed help and those in the car with her were refusing to help her friend.

With tears streaming down her face and her words completely enveloped in emotion, Kim tried to stand up to get into a better position to open the side door and let Tony into the van. Meghan finally turned, pushed Kim back down and held her there with her both of her hands on her shoulders. She didn't say anything. She just held her there.

Jules, who had been sitting on Kim's lap and was now on Emma's very crowded lap, was crying as well. Things went from being fairly tense, like her house used to get before the whole family would leave for vacation, to all of a sudden being outright frightening. She didn't like what was happening, even though she didn't completely understand it either. She didn't know why all those people were so mad and Tony was just too scary with all that red on him. Why couldn't he just wash all that off so that he could get back in the car with the rest of them? Why was he trying to be scary too? She buried her face in Emma's shoulder and chest and cried until the adult's sweatshirt was damp with tears.

Danny, for his part, sat as quietly as he was able. When Jules invaded Emma's lap to accommodate Kim's fit, he simply moved aside and made room. Honestly, it was difficult for him to really do anything else. He was a little stunned by what was going on around him. He knew that they were in trouble and that this could end badly for all of them, though, in truth, he wasn't quite sure what that really meant. In a child's sort of way he understood death but had a hard time grasping the finality of it. Death had been a part of movies and video games that could be watched again and again. Death could be negated by a reset or rewind button and the hero or even the villain was alive again and any mistakes had been washed away. For the time being however, Danny sat quietly and tried to contain the sensation that was building in his stomach. It was the anticipation that struck a rider in the lead car of a roller coaster as it crested its first and most steep peak. He could feel the butterflies trying to escape from his mouth. He just swallowed down the fluttering, decorative moths that were threatening to breach.

Neil pressed the accelerator to the floor and held the steering wheel tightly between his white, straining knuckles. With those things running at him, he hoped he could get enough speed to punch through.

Emma wanted to scream, remembering her previous experience with Officer Ivanoff at the helm. She didn't know if this was a better idea now than it was then. She withheld her protests though not entirely by choice. She was finding it impossible to concentrate enough on one thing to be able to find even the ability for coherent speech. She just tightened her grip on the shiny pistol in her right hand and tried to bury her scream beneath a panicked moan that escaped through tensely sealed lips. The sound resembled a frightened puppy's whimper. It escaped her without her even realizing it until after it had happened. Danny preferred the scream to the moan. It was less unsettling and felt much less like what he'd hear on a roller coaster.

And Officer Ivanoff just sat and stared ahead. He wasn't quite smiling, although the pathetic noises the whore behind him was making were somewhat satisfying, but the emotion evinced in his face wasn't that far off from contentment. His eyes though, despite what was happening all around them, were empty and distant, like he was lost in deep thought or memory. He wasn't entirely sure as to what to believe was happening for certain. He couldn't remember for sure, but he thought he was just in his father's house, and then all of a sudden he was in Anchorage. He was really having a hard time keeping everything straight at the moment. So, knowing that he could grasp onto that woman's discomfort and know that there were still certainties in this world helped to soothe his fears, but it did not vanquish his disorientation.

Jerry, more or less on the floor next to the police officer, kept a watchful eye on him. Malachi made him very uncomfortable especially since his comment about Tony. Jerry didn't like the fact that they were in a pretty fragile situation and they had a guy with them who might be a little psychotic, a religious fundamentalist, and most definitely armed. Jerry kept moving his eyes from the windows all around him to Malachi's hand that was closest to his gun.

The first several ghouls merely bounced off the minivan, their heads thumping horribly against the bumper and side paneling of the vehicle. The vehicle started to struggle and slow as bodies began to pile up beneath its wheels. Neil tried to swerve in and out of open spaces, but the spaces were too few and too small. They were being enveloped. The van struggled to keep moving forward, like a running back being assailed by an opposing defensive line.

When they slowed to but a crawl, Dr. Caldwell looked over and asked through his nearly clinched teeth, "Now?" holding up the key bob.

"A few seconds more. We can't do it too early."

From their assailants, who were trying desperately to attach themselves to the moving vehicle, the van's windows had become smudged and smeared with brownish finger streaks. Below the windows, thankfully, along the vehicle's sides and bumpers, the mess was much more grisly and stomach turning.

When they had all but stopped, Neil shouted, "Nooowwwwwwwwwwww!"

Dr. Caldwell hit the Panic Button and then, above the growling, the grunting, and the screaming they all heard Meghan's alarm begin to howl anew. It demanded and got immediate attention. With the zombies' attention suddenly drawn away from them, there was a lull, of which Neil quickly took advantage by throwing the vehicle into reverse. The van rolled over and pushed aside a few of the things that had tried to close behind them. The vehicle bounced and rocked as it rolled over legs, arms, and torsos, which all cracked and broke beneath its tires.

Emma, with her free left hand, was hugging the children on her lap close against her chest. Jules burrowed her face deeper into Emma's chest and tried to find a song in her head to chase away her fear. She didn't like this one bit and the fact that her mother wasn't there to hold her and tell her that everything was going to be alright made things that much worse.

Due in large part to the distraction of Meghan's alarm, Neil got them free again from the confused mix of stumbling and knotted former humanity. Once clear, he shifted the vehicle back into drive and made a hard and fast detour around the struggling ghouls now conveniently gathered and clumped in the middle of the street. He steered the van through a flat yard and across a couple of driveways and simply drove around the group. Once around, he got them back on the pavement and drove out and away.

A few of the fresher looking corpses tried to pursue, but the van's speed on the clear street made the pursuit on foot all for naught. It wasn't for lack of trying though. Neil watched them continue to chase after them as he got them onto the Old Seward Highway and they dropped out of sight. He knew that they were still following, but that wouldn't matter so long as they could keep moving.

There were stalled and abandoned cars dotting the road, but there were enough gaps here and there that they were able to make their way out onto Huffman Road. The little retail park to their left, once bustling with activity, was bereft of even the most remote signs of life. Even the ravens, the garbage scavenging dumpster-divers of the north, had abandoned the litter-filled parking lots. Discarded newspapers, empty plastic shopping bags, and any other lightweight scraps of a world in decay fluttered on the stiff autumn breezes. There were other piles of garbage scattered here and there, but then Neil realized, after looking at one that was nearer to the road that the piles of garbage were actually decomposing bodies. He couldn't figure out how there could be dead bodies, considering what happened to a body that met its demise at the hands or, more to the point, teeth of one of those things. Whether he could understand it or not, there they lay. He thought to himself, just drive. None of it much mattered anymore. He just needed to drive and put all of it behind them. As if that was even possible. He drove them straight ahead into the mouth of the great unknown.

Just when he thought there was no comfort left in the world, Meghan's hands, no longer restraining Kim, found their way to Neil's shoulders. They touched him lightly, massaging his tensed neck and soothing his doubts and fears even if only for the briefest of moments. She leaned forward and whispered, "Thank you."